A DEAL
BEFORE THE ALTAR

BY
RACHAEL THOMAS

MILLS &
BOON

Published in Great Britain 2014
by Mills & Boon, an imprint of Harlequin (UK) Limited,
Eton House, 18-24 Paradise Road, Richmond, Surrey, TW9 1SR

© 2014 Rachael Thomas

ISBN: 978-0-263-90907-4

Harlequin (UK) Limited's policy is to use papers that are natural,
renewable and recyclable products and made from wood grown in
sustainable forests. The logging and manufacturing processes conform
to the legal environmental regulations of the country of origin.

Printed and bound in Spain
by Blackprint CPI, Barcelona

A DEAL
BEFORE THE ALTAR

To my family and friends, who have supported me always
as I've pursued my dream,
and to the wonderful friendships I've made along the way.

CHAPTER ONE

GEORGINA ENTERED THE sleek luxury of the office and knew she was being watched. Her every step scrutinised by a man who was revered and feared by businessmen and women alike.

'Ms Henshaw.' His deep voice, with a hint of accent, was firm and commanding. 'I don't think I need to ask why you are here.'

He leant against his desk, arms folded across his broad chest, as if he'd already decided he didn't want to hear what she had to say. His black hair gleamed, but the intensity in his eyes nearly robbed her of the ability to speak.

'I'm sure you don't, Mr Ramirez.' She injected as much firmness into her voice as she could, determined she wouldn't be dismissed before she'd said all she had to say. 'You are, after all, the cause of the problem.'

'Am I indeed?' Santos Lopez Ramirez locked his gaze with hers and for a moment she almost lost her nerve. Almost.

She studied his face, looking for a hint of compassion, but there was nothing. His mouth was set in a firm line that highlighted the harsh angles of his cheekbones, softened only slightly by his tanned complexion. His jaw was cleanshaven, but she didn't miss the way he clenched it, as if biting back his words.

'You know you are.' She paused briefly before continuing. 'You are the one person who is preventing Emma and Carlo from doing what they want.'

'So what are you going to do about it, Ms Henshaw?'

As he raised his brows in question a flutter of nerves took flight in her stomach. But now was the time to be the woman the world thought she was—the cold and manipulative woman who took exactly what she wanted in life and discarded what she didn't.

'I will do whatever it takes to make it happen, Mr Ramirez.'

The butterflies dissipated as she thought of Emma, of all the dreams of a fairytale wedding her younger sister so often spoke about. Her own ideas of love and happiness had long since been shattered, but she wanted her sister to find that dream.

'That's a very bold statement.'

Bold. Stupid. It didn't matter what he thought. All she cared about was Emma's happiness—happiness was something neither of them had experienced much of in recent years.

'I'm a very bold woman, Mr Ramirez.'

He smiled. An indolent smile that tugged at the corners of his mouth. Her breath caught in her throat and nerves almost swarmed over her as he unfolded his arms and took a purposeful step towards her.

'I admire that in a woman.'

Tall and unyielding, he stood before her. And despite the spacious office, the wall of windows and the sparse furnishings, he dominated the room.

She stood her ground, refusing to move, to be intimidated. 'Your admiration is not the reason I'm here.'

'I don't have time for games, Ms Henshaw.'

'I have a deal to put to you, Mr Ramirez.' He couldn't

dismiss her yet. It had been hard enough getting past his secretary, and she didn't intend to waste the opportunity.

'A deal?'

'I meant what I said.' She spoke firmly, determined he should never know just how anxious she was, how desperate to achieve her aim. 'I will do whatever it takes.'

Santos took in the determined jut of the brunette's chin. She looked so arrogantly sure of herself that he wondered if she was going to start the Paso Doble right there in his office.

Lust hurtled through his body at the images such thoughts brought to mind.

'And why would you want to do that?'

Santos returned to his chair and sat down, his gaze running over her body. The charcoal skirt and jacket, although professional and businesslike, did little to disguise her womanly figure. The tantalising hint of a lace camisole beneath the jacket caught his eye, but it was the heels she wore that stole the show. Her designer leopard print heels not only spoke volumes about the real woman, but showcased the most fantastic pair of legs he'd seen in ages. He was entranced, but it was the attitude radiating from her glorious body that really intrigued him.

'Emma is my sister and I want her to be happy.'

The intensity of her gaze as she spoke only aroused his interest further.

'I'll do anything to achieve that.'

He rose from his chair, his body suddenly restless, to stand in front of the floor-to-ceiling windows of his office. He surveyed the view of London glinting in the autumn sunshine, recalling all he'd discovered about the sister of quiet and demure Emma, the woman his half-brother Carlo was currently dating. A situation that had thrown everything into turmoil.

This woman certainly had a reputation. Widowed at twenty-three, and having been left a substantial fortune, she now led a socialite lifestyle and was never short of male company. A mercenary woman, if the circumstances of her marriage were to be believed.

'And just how far are you prepared to go in the name of sisterly love?'

Behind him he heard her intake of breath and knew he'd touched a nerve. A stab of desire shot through him as he imagined her sighing in pleasure as he kissed her. Quickly he regained control. Now was not a good time to find himself attracted to a woman—especially one with such a tarnished and scandalous reputation. He had a business to run. One that was a contentious issue between himself and Carlo. One he had to find a solution to quickly. Time was running out.

'As I have already said, Mr Ramirez, I will do whatever it takes.' Her voice had a slightly husky quality to it, which threatened to undo his control, so he remained focused on the view of London a moment longer.

Finally he turned to face her, strode across the thick carpet until he stood at her side, his right arm almost touching her shoulder. He looked sideways down at her, catching her light floral scent as he did so. Not the sort usually favoured by a woman of her reputation—it was soft and very feminine.

'So you agree with their plans to marry…your sister and my brother?'

She stood firm, like a soldier on parade being inspected by a commanding officer. He walked slowly round behind her, admiration building. She didn't flinch, didn't move. His gaze was drawn to the streaks of fiery red which entwined in her hair and again he thought of her in his bed, hair wildly fanned out across the pillow.

'Why shouldn't they get married?'

Her words drew him sharply back. 'They are young,' he said quietly, and walked away from her. Being close distracted him, took his mind from the current problem to more primal matters. 'Too young.'

'They are in love.' The words flew at him across the room with such passion that he stopped to look at her, wondering if she was as indifferent and in control as she wanted him to think. He looked at her beautiful face, the firm set of her full lips and the haughty rise of her brows. Had he just imagined that spark of passion? Conjured it up because of the direction his thoughts had gone? He must have done. As she stood before him she was not only sculpted from ice but frozen to the core.

A challenge indeed.

'And you believe in love, do you?' All through his younger years he'd been introduced to an endless stream of his father's girlfriends. Then as a teenager he'd watched from the sidelines as his father had fallen under the spell of a younger woman. The love they'd shared and later bestowed on Carlo, his new brother, had been incomprehensible to him. It had done little to instil ideas of love and happiness in him.

'About as much as you do.'

Her gaze met his, stubbornly holding it, provoking him to deny it.

'Very perceptive, Ms Henshaw. We are, then, kindred spirits, able to enjoy the opposite sex without the drama of emotional attachment.'

This was always the attitude he'd adopted, and one that had begun to feel less and less favourable. But the idea of being so captivated by a woman, so completely under her spell it would make a man turn his back on his son, was even less appealing.

'Put like that, then, yes, I suppose we are.'

Georgina cringed inwardly, knowing exactly what he was referring to. Was he really going to drag up her past, use it as a reason to stop his brother from marrying Emma? She wouldn't let him—not when she now knew the real reason he didn't want them to marry. She had to change his mind.

For a moment her nerves almost got the better of her. There was only one option she could think of to secure her sister's happiness, and although it didn't sit well with her she had to persuade him it was possible.

'What exactly is it you want, Ms Henshaw?'

A distanced, almost bored tone had entered his voice and she watched him stalk back to the windows, looking more like a caged animal than a businessman.

'I want to put a business proposition to you.'

He turned instantly, his interest piqued, and she stifled a smile of triumph. She was now talking his language. Business was what made this man tick. That was obvious.

'A proposition? You?'

He moved back to his desk and gestured her to sit, the muscles of his arm rippling beneath his white shirt snagging her attention. Mentally she shook herself. Getting distracted by his good looks would not help her through this. And hadn't she told herself months ago that relationships were not what she needed?

'I'd prefer to stand,' she said firmly, not missing the quirk of his dark brows.

'As you wish.'

He sat behind his desk, his dark eyes watching her. She wouldn't let him intimidate her. She had to remain as calm and detached as possible. So much was riding on her being able to deliver her proposition in an efficient, businesslike manner.

'I want my sister to be happy, and Carlo makes her happy.' She tried to keep her voice steady and devoid of emotion. This hard businessman obviously believed all that was written about her in the press. He believed she was cast from the same mould as him. 'From my understanding of the situation, there is only one solution.'

He didn't say a word, waiting for her to continue. His silence unnerved her, but she had to stay strong, remain focused.

Quickly she pressed on. 'I know about the condition in your father's will.'

'You are very well informed of my affairs, Ms Henshaw, but I fail to see what business of yours that is.'

His hard expression gave her a glimpse of the formidable businessman he was. She'd done her research on him. 'I know you have built your business up to the international concern it is today since your father passed away, and that once either you or Carlo marry the business will pass solely to that brother.' She paused, almost wanting to give up as she looked at him, his dark eyes as bleak as a starless night.

'Full marks for research,' he said, his voice as emotionless as she hoped hers was.

It had been Emma who had told her about the condition of the will. She'd sobbed for the loss of her dreams of marrying the man she loved, dreams of living happily ever after with Carlo, just because of the greed of his elder brother.

'I also know Carlo doesn't share your appetite for success. He has little or no interest in the business, wanting only to live a normal life married to my sister.'

'A *normal* life?'

She knew he was stalling, being evasive. Wouldn't she hate it if he picked apart her private affairs? But she had to carry on before she lost all confidence in her plan. For Emma she had to do it, just as she'd had to five years ago.

'A life that isn't centred on a business but one that is centred on a happy family home.' The words flowed from her with practised ease.

'And an example of that would be your own family, would it?'

She felt her eyes widen, shocked he'd brought it up. 'I see you have done your own research, Mr Ramirez, but my parents' marriage has nothing to do with Emma and Carlo.'

'I have no wish for my family name to be joined by marriage to a woman's whose mother is an alcoholic and whose father has been absent so long nobody knows where he is.'

'So it has nothing to do with your power-hungry need to take the business from Carlo by preventing this marriage?' Her heartbeat was rising and her emotions were beginning to take over. She had to remain composed.

'They have sent you here to plead their case, have they?'

He glowered at her. But her last words seemed only to have bounced off his tough exterior. She took a deep breath, wanting to appear poised before she spoke again.

He laced his long tanned fingers together in front of him on the desk in a relaxed fashion, but Georgina knew he was anything but relaxed. The firm set of his broad shoulders gave that away. He was confident, self-assured and powerful.

'On the contrary, Mr Ramirez, they have no idea I'm here and I want it to stay that way.'

RACHAEL THOMAS   15

One dark brow quirked up, but he said nothing.

'I can see only one way to secure their happiness...'
She paused, refusing to be drawn. 'And to satisfy your
insatiable need for business success.'

He leant forward at his desk. 'And that is?'

'You get married first, inherit the business, and leave
them to enjoy a happy married life together.'

As he looked at her his handsome face set in a mask
so emotionless she blinked in shock. Did this man not
have any compassion in his heart?

'As you seem to have it all worked out, who do you
suggest I marry?' The question came out slowly, as if he
was sure he'd foiled her plan.

She took a deep breath and looked directly into his
eyes. She mustn't show any nerves, any fear. He was like
a predatory lion and she knew he'd smell it.

'Me.'

There—she'd said it. And now she had she wanted to
bolt like a frightened animal. He didn't say a word. Not a
trace of emotion could be seen on his face. Silence hung
between them, and a tension so taut she thought it was
going to snap with a crack at any moment.

Shock rocked through Santos as he listened to her ridiculous proposition. It was the last thing he'd expected to
hear, but then her reputation should have given him fore-
warning. She already had one marriage behind her—one
that had made her a very wealthy woman indeed. And if
rumour was to be believed it had not been a love-match.

'Why, exactly, would I wish to get married? And to
you, of all women?'

His voice was hard, his accent suddenly more pro-
nounced. He sounded dangerous.

Briefly Santos saw pain flash across her face, saw the

curling of her manicured fingers and wished the words unsaid. Marriage was the one thing he wanted to avoid at all costs, but even though his legal team were working on a solution he had to consider the option. If he wanted to save his business, and the last five years of hard work since his father had first become ill, he might actually have to take a wife. So wouldn't this woman, who had so willingly walked into the lion's den, be the perfect choice? Costly, maybe, if her track record was anything to go by, but he could deal with that.

'It wouldn't be a marriage in the true sense of the word.'

Her words, spoken with conviction, dragged his attention back to her face.

'And what is that?'

'A marriage for love, of course—like the one your brother and my sister wish to make. A commitment for life.' Her words flowed freely, and once again he thought he heard a spark of passion.

Suspiciously he looked at her as he sat back again in his chair. 'You are not looking for love, Ms Henshaw?'

'Not at all, Mr Ramirez. I only want my sister's happiness. I will do anything to achieve that. Once they are married we can annul our marriage and go separate ways.

Santos considered this wild suggestion more seriously. Would it hurt to go along with it for now—to have another option if his legal team were unable to sort out an alternative?

'And you would want what, exactly, from this *marriage*?' His mind raced. On a business level it made perfect sense. He would finally have the security of inheriting the business he'd built up and would have done his duty by his brother, freeing Carlo of obligations he had little or no interest in.

'I want nothing from you other than our names on a marriage certificate. Once that is done we need not see each other. We just apply for an annulment.'

Her voice had hardened and his past rushed back at him. He saw the teenager who had hardly grieved for his controlling mother. Felt the pain as his father eventually remarried and moved on with a loving and kind woman whom Santos had resented. A woman who had changed his father, almost taking him away from his firstborn with the power of her love.

'I find that hard to believe. You must want something.' Experience had taught him that. Everyone wanted something. Everyone had a price.

'Nothing more than I've already stated.'

Her cool, calm words sounded believable.

Santos thought of the conditions of the will and gritted his teeth against the memory of the day he'd realised what his manipulative father had done. It seemed this attractive woman knew a lot about the will, but she didn't know it all. She hadn't mentioned the other conditions that he would have to meet before finally inheriting. It wasn't as simple as marriage.

'I require more than that. My wife, when I take one, will be a wife in every sense of the word.'

Did she really think he was going to accept her proposition meekly, without attaching his own conditions? If he had to get married he'd rather do it for business than become as vulnerable as his father had after his second marriage. There was also the matter that he was a hot-blooded male and this woman had stirred his blood the second she'd walked proudly into his office.

Santos watched as realisation dawned on her pretty face, followed by defeat. But he said nothing more. To do so now would be to show his hand. He would never give away the fact that he actually saw her proposition as a serious option—his back-up plan.

'I can't do that.' She gasped the words out, her face whitening before his eyes.

'Then your very first words to me were lies.'

Part of him felt relieved. She hadn't really been serious. But another part of him, the deal-chaser, wanted this—but on his terms. Marriage would not only secure the business but would put a stop to the endless rounds of parties. It would enhance his image in the business world, giving him what appeared to be a happy marriage, and it would mean he didn't have to get emotionally involved. Something he avoided at all costs.

She still hadn't spoken so he carried on, pushing forward his conditions, turning it completely to his advantage. 'That is the only deal I'm prepared to make.'

Georgina's heart sank. Was he seriously suggesting a real marriage—one that would entail her being at his side publicly *and* sleeping in his bed at night?

'We know nothing of each other.' She grabbed at the first thing that came to mind.

'On the contrary, Georgina. I think we both know enough.'

The use of her name sent a warm tingle down her spine. His gaze fixed on hers so intently she felt as if he was physically holding her captive. Her pulse-rate leapt, then beat hard as she thought of spending the night in his bed, of being his wife in every sense of the word.

She couldn't banish the image of him with one of his model-like women hanging on his arm. Would such a man as Santos Ramirez even want to be seen publicly with her? Worse still, would he find her lacking as a lover? No, *lover* wasn't the right word. Would he find her lacking as a sexual partner?

'I know that the world would never be fooled into thinking we had married for any other reason than convenience.' She clutched awkwardly at excuses as she still struggled to take in what he wanted.

'And that would be because you have already been married and widowed purely for financial gain.'

Pain lanced through her as she thought of Richard Henshaw—the man she'd married because she had been genuinely fond of him. The same man who had given her stability and security in her life for the first time ever. In that moment she hated Santos more than any other man for bringing Richard into it.

'No.' Her voice filled with entreaty. 'Because I am nothing like the type of woman you date.'

He raised a brow, and a slight smile teased at the corners of his lips. 'As far as people would know I'd have become besotted with you exactly *because* you are not like any woman I have ever dated.'

'Would you really want people to think that instead of thinking we were married in name only to keep your business?'

'I have no intention of anyone ever thinking I have married for business gain only.' He looked steadily at her. 'Especially Carlo.'

Georgina couldn't take it in. Her whole plan had been turned upside down. He'd taken complete and utter control of the situation and turned it into something she just couldn't think of doing.

'How is that achievable?'

She struggled to comprehend how Emma would ever believe she had married such a man simply because she wanted to. Not now Emma knew all about her first marriage and the reasons behind it.

'You said that nobody knows you are here—is that not true?'

'No, nobody,' she replied, trying to grasp where this was leading.

'Good,' he said, and stood up, making her feel small and insignificant as he moved around his desk to stand before her once more. 'I will host a party tomorrow evening, to which you and Emma are invited.'

'How is that going to help?' Georgina couldn't figure out where he was going with this.

He smiled. A lazy smile that did nothing to hide his amusement at the situation. 'We won't be able to leave each other alone; the attraction will be obvious to all there. Then we will spend the entire weekend together, maybe longer, after which we shall make the announcement.'

The tone of his voice had changed, giving it a warm depth, and she had the distinct impression that if he was really attracted to her she would be unable to resist. A tingle shimmied down her spine, causing her pulse-rate to leap—which had nothing to do with anxiety and everything to do with the dark and possibly dangerous man who watched her intently.

'Okay,' she said quickly, aware that her voice had become a husky whisper. She wanted to push on with her plans but hoped she could change his mind later. A real marriage surely wasn't necessary. 'We'll do it your way.'

'There was never any doubt about that, *querida*.'

CHAPTER TWO

GEORGINA'S ANXIETY LEVELS had risen tenfold since entering the hotel where Santos was having his impromptu party. Her sister, who was so excited, believing a party meant there was hope for her and Carlo to be married, had vanished from her side the moment they arrived. Georgina now felt conspicuous as she stood just inside the doorway of the hotel room.

'*Buenas noches,* Ms Henshaw.'

She looked up at Santos, her breath catching as he moved closer to her. He was immaculately dressed in a dark suit and tie, the white of his shirt enhancing his attractive tan. The smile on his lips was warm and welcoming. That same warmth reached his eyes as he took her hand. The touch of his fingers as he lightly held hers made her shiver, as if a feather had been trailed down her spine.

Speak, she told herself firmly. *Don't let his act of attraction distract you.*

'Good evening, Mr Ramirez,' she said, injecting firmness into her voice as she remembered they were not yet supposed to have met. She certainly didn't want Emma to discover what she was about to do. 'It is a pleasure to meet you at last.'

He quirked a brow, and she wondered if she'd gone too far, but around her they were already drawing speculative gazes. It seemed to Georgina that the elite of London society were here—and all at his request.

'Please, call me Santos,' he said as he lifted her hand to his lips.

Her stomach did a strange flutter as those lips brushed sensuously over the back of her hand. Stunned into silence, she was mesmerised by his dark hair as he lowered his head. The barely controlled waves of shiny black hair looked so inviting she wondered what it would feel like to run her fingers through it. Then he straightened, towering over her once more, his gaze locking with hers.

Don't go there, she warned herself, and tried to pull back her hand, but his fingers tightened on hers. A sexy smile spread across his lips and she dragged in a ragged breath, then swallowed hard. What was she doing, allowing this man to get to her?

'The pleasure is mine.' His words were deep and uneven. He didn't let her hand go, instead forcing her to stay, so that she could do nothing other than stand there. She looked into the ever darkening depths of his eyes and felt a sizzle of awareness slide over her like the slow thaw of mountain snow. Shy and flustered was something she'd never felt—but, far worse, she knew she was already out of her depth. How was she ever going to get through the evening when he turned on charm like this?

She would because she had to. She was doing this for Emma's happiness. She clutched her bag, thinking of the few essentials she'd slipped into it, knowing she wasn't going to be returning home that night.

She smiled, more to herself than anyone else, determined not to let this man's charisma knock her off balance. It was all for show, and if he could do it then so could she.

'Something is amusing you?' His fingers traced a slow,

teasing circle on the palm of her hand, making tingles race along her arm. She wanted to pull away, wanted to break the contact, yet couldn't. Somewhere deep inside her something stirred—an emotion long since locked away.

'I was merely admiring your charm.' She smiled up at him, pulling herself closer against him. It felt flirty. Dangerous. 'I'm sure women just drop at your feet.'

He laughed. A soft rumble that made her tremble. Instinctively she tried to pull her hand free. Again his fingers tightened and his eyes darkened, and for a moment her eyes locked with his. She drew in a quick breath as she saw the sparks of desire within those dark depths. Her body responded to the primal call of his as heady heat thundered around her.

'That is always my intention, *querida*.'

He smiled down at her, letting her hand go so that she felt suddenly bereft of his contact—like a ship torn from its anchor to drift in the harbour.

'Champagne?'

She blinked, not quite able to keep up with his train of thought. Glancing around her, she caught her sister's eye as she chatted with other guests, Carlo at her side. Emma looked radiant and happy, and Georgina knew there was no going back now. Just as she had done five years ago, she had to put Emma first. She'd done it once, and she could do it again, but Emma must never know.

'Champagne would be lovely,' she purred, being as flirtatious as she possibly could. Maybe a little champagne was just what she needed to boost her confidence.

With his hand in the small of her back she moved into the room, aware of the curious glances being directed their way. Santos handed her a flute of champagne, but her head was becoming light, as if she'd already had several glasses of the bubbly liquid. She couldn't quite believe how this handsome and powerful businessman was able to make her feel so special, so fresh and alive. His charm offensive was potent, making her feel unique and, worse than that, desired. If this was how he was going to play out their planned public scene of attraction she would have to be careful, remind herself it was all an act. Because right now it felt very real. And she liked it.

Santos couldn't help but watch Georgina as she sipped her champagne. The need to act as if he were attracted to her had gone out of the window the moment she'd entered the room. He'd heard the hush, felt the ripple of interest, and had been as mesmerised by her as every other man in the room.

Still looking as proud and defiant as she had yesterday in his office, she'd stood framed in the doorway. The jade silk of her dress skimmed over her body, neither revealing nor concealing her curves. A black wrap hung loosely off her shoulders, and he'd been unable to take his eyes off the creamy expanse of her skin, broken only by the thin jade straps. Her neck was bare of any jewellery—something many of the women he knew couldn't carry off.

Even if he hadn't had to go up to her and start the charade of attraction he would have wanted to. The same kick of lust he'd felt yesterday had stirred in his veins once again, propelling him towards her. As he'd taken her hand, enjoying the softness of her skin, he had known he wanted her.

'Your plan is working.' He leant down and whispered against her hair, the fresh scent of it invading his senses, making his pulse throb with unquenched desire.

She pulled back from him, confusion filling her eyes, her fingers clutching tightly to her glass. 'It is?'

He heard the uncertainty in her voice and had the strangest desire to stroke his fingers down her cheek. An affectionate gesture he'd never normally think of making. Just what was it about this woman that stirred something unknown deep within him?

'With your dedication to the role, how could anyone question what they are seeing?' She turned away, exchanging her empty glass for another bubble-filled one.

The brittleness of her words reminded him just who he was dealing with. Georgina Henshaw was an avaricious woman who, with one marriage already behind her, could play his game with as much detachment as he employed.

He watched her beautiful yet emotionless face as she scanned the room, her eyes finally resting on her sister. With a sternness that would have become any teacher her gaze followed Emma as she moved across the room, until she nestled herself against his brother.

Unable to stop himself from watching the loving moment, he saw how his brother looked down at Emma. Saw the open adoration in the young woman's eyes. Even as Carlo dipped his head and kissed her he couldn't avert his gaze. Whatever it was between them was so powerful he felt it from the other side of the room. Just as he had done as a youth, when Carlo's mother had first met his father, he felt excluded. It was almost as if he'd gone back in time, watching Carlo grow strong from his mother's love while he could only look on.

'They make a good couple, don't they?'

Georgina's words dragged him back from a past he rarely visited. For a moment he was disorientated.

'They don't have to marry to prove that.'

He couldn't keep the harshness from his words. Beside him Georgina stiffened, as if she was taking a step back from him. He forced his mind to more pleasant thoughts—like the way the woman at his side stirred his desires like no other.

'I hope you aren't going back on our deal, Mr Ramirez?'

He deflected her sharp-toned words with a smile. 'Santos,' he said softly, placing his arm across her shoulders and pulling her body against his, relishing the warmth of it. 'I think you should call me Santos. If you want this to work.'

He looked down into her upturned face. Her eyes darkened until they reminded him of the depths of a forest. Her full lips parted slightly and he felt the heavy tug of desire.

He wanted her.

Slowly he lowered his head and brushed his lips over hers. Her breath mingled with his, warming his mouth, and he imagined the sensation of her sighing in pleasure. This was going to be a *very* interesting night.

Briefly her lips responded. Softening beneath his. And his whole body suddenly ached for hers. It was stronger than the heady lust that usually coursed through his blood when he kissed a woman. This was potent. Vibrant and alive. It was more powerful than anything he'd known before.

Georgina's body heated as his lips touched hers, the contact so light it almost didn't happen. Involuntarily she closed her eyes as the liquid warmth of desire slid over her. She swayed closer to him, felt his arm, strong and firm, draw her closer.

She knew there and then that he had power over her. He had the ability to stir emotions she never again wanted to explore, and she would have to be on her guard.

Her fingers clutched the stem of the glass in her hand as she hardened herself against what she was feeling. This wasn't for real. This was all an act. And if she didn't keep that in mind she'd make a fool of herself, because at this moment in time she wanted nothing more than to be kissed by Santos.

Not this light, lingering kiss. After several years without experiencing the intimacy of any kiss she knew he'd awakened something deep within her. She wanted more. Her body hungered for passion. To her horror, she realised her body hungered for *him*.

But she couldn't let that happen. She had to stay in control—not just of herself, but of the situation. Never could she allow herself to become a woman so desperate for love that she'd beg a man to stay, as her mother had done to her father. In Santos she recognised the same inability to commit to a relationship her father had possessed. He would be the worst man for her to give her heart to.

No, to allow Santos to know just how easily he could stir her hidden and unexplored desires would be fatal.

She pulled away from him and looked into his smouldering eyes. He was good. Nobody could question what he was thinking right now. He looked as if he wanted to ravish her right there in the middle of the party.

A tingle raced around her at the thought and her breathing deepened. It was as if her body was working in opposition to her heart and her head, and it was winning.

She flirted back at him, ignoring the heavy ache of her limbs and the throb of desire deep inside her. 'Santos, that was…' She paused and looked beyond him into the throng of partygoers who mingled around them, looked to her sister. 'Amazing,' she finished, hoping he'd think the husky note in her voice was part of her act and not something she had little or no control over—a reaction to him.

'Amazing, huh?'

His voice was deeper and his accent, which had only been a hint before, much stronger. He sounded sexy. *Too* sexy.

'Definitely. Emma looks so shocked. I'm certain she'll believe there is something between us.' She moved against him as she spoke, felt the firmness of his body and tried to ignore the sizzle of electricity zipping around hers.

'And what about you, *querida*? Do you believe it?'

He smiled down at her, pulling her just a little closer, so that she could feel her breasts pressing against his chest. Her breath caught in her throat and for a moment she couldn't say a word.

Focus, she reminded herself. *Focus on why you're even here with him.*

'I believe we look convincing.' She hated the way her voice stammered, and to hide it lifted her chin and raised a brow at him.

He laughed. A soft sound she felt rumbling against her. It was all too close, too personal. She tried to step back from him but he pressed his hand firmly into the small of her back, bringing her hip close against him.

She gasped as she felt the hardness of his arousal, and nerves made her heart beat wildly—so hard she could feel the pulse in her neck throbbing. His dark eyes, smouldering with desire, met hers.

'I too am convinced.'

His voice was a harsh whisper as he spoke against her ear, his breath blowing on her neck, making it tingle.

'I am also convinced that now would be a good time to leave this damned party.'

She turned her head towards him, intending to speak, to try and douse the fire that had ignited between them. A fire she could never allow to burn. Her cheek touched his as he lowered his head and, following some kind of instinct she'd never before experienced, she moved until his lips were against hers.

Briefly her gaze locked with his, then her eyelids fluttered closed as the pressure of his lips met hers. The kiss was hard, demanding much more. She wound her arms around his neck, one hand still clutching her empty champagne flute, and gave herself up to the mastery of this man's kiss. Her lips and her body asked for more and he responded, making her heart thump hard.

His tongue slid into her mouth, entwining with hers. He tasted wild and untamed. She sighed, making him deepen the kiss, and he began to invade every cell of her body with a heady desire she'd never known before.

Heaven help her, she wanted this man. Wanted him in a way she hadn't known was possible.

Just when she thought she couldn't remain standing against him any longer he broke the kiss. She slid her arms down slowly from his neck and he took the glass from her hand, putting it on a nearby table. Cool air rushed around her as their bodies parted and she felt exposed, naked, as if everyone in the room would be able to see just how much her body wanted his.

Santos's gaze slid over her, just as it had done when she'd entered the room, but this time her skin sizzled. When it lingered on her breasts her knees weakened and breathing was suddenly the hardest thing to do. She was transfixed, unable to move, unable to hide from his open desire.

Around them the noise of the party slowly came back

to her and she was thankful that they were not alone. What would she have done if they were?

She'd have made a big mistake, that was what. She would have allowed passion and champagne to take over, allowed them to destroy everything, exposing emotions and leaving her vulnerable. She'd seen it with her mother, knew the consequences, and had promised herself she'd never allow that to happen to her.

'We leave now.'

His voice, though still deep and throaty, radiated total command and, afraid hers would sound weak and trembling, she nodded in agreement.

With his hand possessively in the small of her back he propelled her towards the door. Partygoers stepped aside for them. Envious glances from women came her way. The cool façade she lived behind slipped firmly back into place. She lifted her chin, smiled, and walked proudly at Santos's side.

What would they think if they knew the truth? Would they gasp in shock at the calculated plan she was acting out?

'Georgie?' Emma's voice filtered through the defensive wall she'd quickly rebuilt, despite the hum of her body.

She looked into her sister's face and saw genuine happiness. It shone from her eyes so brightly that she knew she was doing the right thing. She touched Emma's arm and gave her a secretive smile. The smile of a woman who was being swept away by the most magnetic man she'd ever met.

'I'll call you in the morning.'

Emma's smile widened and she looked from her to Santos and back again. 'Okay.' She grinned and turned to leave, obviously in a hurry to tell Carlo.

'Let's go,' Georgina said, without looking at Santos. The taste of deception was strong in her mouth.

'I like it.'

His voice purred like a big cat content to take it easy for a while. He led her out of the noise of the party into the hotel foyer. The lights were brighter—too bright—as if she was now under his spotlight. His gaze slid down her again, desire still sparking in his eyes despite the latent control in his voice.

'*What* do you like?' she questioned sharply as he began to lead her out onto the streets. She shivered against the cold autumn air.

'Georgie.'

Emma's pet name for her sounded so exotic on his lips—sexy, even. Her body heated despite the wind, which blew her hair quickly into disarray. She combed her fingers through it, gathering it at her neck, trying to prevent herself from becoming a totally dishevelled mess.

'I prefer Georgina,' she said, trying to ignore the way her body hummed as he took her hand and pulled her close against him. Was this what it was like to be protected?

Minutes later she was in the back of his chauffeur-driven car. The light from the streetlamps cast a glow around the interior and she glanced at Santos, startled to find he was watching her intently.

She looked down at her hands clasped in her lap, unable to look into the heat of his eyes.

'You are a very beautiful woman.'

Georgina tensed. This wasn't supposed to be happening. 'You can drop the act now.' Her words were stiff and she looked up at his face. The angles of his cheekbones were severe in the ever-changing light.

'I'm enjoying the role.' His deep voice seemed to ripple around the car, sending pinpricks of heat rushing over her. 'And you never know who may be listening or watching.'

Georgina glanced at the chauffeur, who appeared to be concentrating on driving. She heard Santos laugh softly and her gaze flew to meet his once more. He really was charming—but on a lethal level. Somewhere deep inside her she recognised him as the kind of man who could hurt her or, worse, destroy her. He was the same type of devil-may-care man her mother had fallen for time and time again, and exactly like her father.

'You don't really think I'll buy that, do you?' She raised a brow at him, infusing indifference into her body with each syllable.

Cool and aloof. That was the protection she needed.

'My staff are nothing but discreet,' he replied as the car came to a stop outside some very exclusive riverside apartments.

'That is a relief—but then I suppose I'm just another on a very long list as far as they are concerned.' The haughty demeanour she routinely hid behind sounded in her voice, and from the look on his face, the frown that furrowed his brow, she knew she'd scored a direct hit.

With one final look at her he got out of the car, almost instantly appearing at her door. He held out his hand for her, but the look on his face suggested he was far from happy. For a moment she was worried. Had she pushed things just a little too far, taunting him like that? A man like him was used to people pandering to his ego.

She had the sudden urge to bolt past him and run away. Reason followed swiftly. She wouldn't help her sister like that, and the shoes she was wearing certainly hadn't been created for running.

'If you want to drop this charade you can go home

now.' His voice was rough, edged with exasperation. 'But just remember, *querida,* it was your idea.'

He was right. She had started this and she would finish it—but only when she knew her sister could marry the man she loved without any implications from this power-hungry man who now stood waiting for her, looking devastatingly sexy. Did he really mean to keep this up, even in private?

For a moment she wondered if she'd already done enough. They'd been seen leaving the party together. Then she remembered Emma's smile, the hope that had shone from her eyes. Georgina realised that it didn't matter what anyone else thought, whether they believed their whirlwind romance was real. It only mattered what Emma thought. There was no way she could let her sister think that yet again she was marrying to secure her future. Emma was all she cared about.

She could do this—even if it meant continuing with the charade of attraction.

Taking his hand, she stepped out of the car and looked up at the tall modern building. She'd never given any thought to where he might live, but the clean, precise lines of this apartment block didn't surprise her.

'I suppose you have the top floor, complete with river views?'

'Very perceptive of you.'

His voice had lowered to a steely tone, interwoven with charm, and her stomach fluttered irrationally.

'It seems you *do* know something about me after all.'

Yes, I do. I know too much. I know you have an abundance of charm and the ability to break a woman's heart.

'It was merely an observation.' Georgina kept the words light as he gestured her towards the entrance of the building. She was beginning to feel disorientated by him, by his seductive tone and sexy smiles. She couldn't allow that to happen. As far as she was concerned once his name was on their marriage certificate and her sister was married all contact would be severed. She had no intention of becoming a *real* wife. Whatever motivation was behind that absurd request she would find a way out of it. She had to.

The lift doors closed on them with expensive silence and as they were taken upwards she kept her eyes straight ahead, watching the doors, not daring to look at him or at their reflection, which seemed to mock her from all sides. She could feel the intensity of his gaze, but refused to meet it. She didn't dare. He was still acting the part of an attracted and attentive man and it was beginning to stir emotions she'd long since locked away.

She almost let out a sigh of relief as the lift doors opened. The opulence of the corridor wasn't lost on her. He wrapped his arm around her, so her elbow nestled in the palm of his hand, and she moved towards the door of his apartment, a sense of dread filling her.

'Do we really need to take it this far?' The words left her in a rush, before she'd had time to consider them.

He stopped outside the white double doors to his apartment, his arm still around her, keeping her close. She looked up at him, desperate to keep calm. He mustn't know just how unnerved he made her feel.

'Yes—if you want authenticity you need to be seen leaving here tomorrow morning.' Amusement lightened his eyes before he turned to open the doors.

'We could have just stayed at the hotel...' She clutched at the idea, not daring to cross the threshold, not wanting to be alone with him—especially on his territory.

'On the contrary.' He smiled that heart-stopping smile that could very easily make her think she was the only woman he saw, the only woman he wanted. 'To bring you here gives a clear message to everyone who knows me—including my brother.'

With his arm firmly around her, he walked into the apartment. She had no choice but to go too. Her heels clicked on a marble floor and the low lighting hinted at a very sparse and masculine living space.

'I don't understand…' The words rushed out on an unsteady breath as he finally moved away from her. At least she could breathe properly, now he wasn't so close.

Dropping his keys onto a table, he took off his jacket and tossed it over the back of a large black leather sofa. Unable to keep her eyes off him, she watched as he loosened his tie and unbuttoned the top of his shirt. Dark tanned skin drew her eyes and she had to force herself to look away.

'I *never* bring a woman back to my apartment.'

The implication of his words sank in. He was giving a very clear message—not just to Carlo, but to her. He wanted the business so badly he was prepared not only to accept her proposal of marriage, but to do everything to make it look real. Even appear to cast aside his womanising reputation and ways and take her as his wife.

'I should be honoured, then,' she replied flippantly, in an attempt to hide her thoughts.

He might be able to discard the way he lived for the sake of his business, but she couldn't quite let slip the distant demeanour *she* hid behind. After all, it wasn't a business she was doing it for, but the love of her sister.

'The first woman to spend a night here with you?'

Santos flicked on a light, wanting to see Georgina's face better. In fact he wanted to see more than just her face. All evening her soft skin had teased his senses—so much so that he'd done the one thing he never did with any woman. He'd kissed her publicly. Not just a light brush of lips on lips either, but a desire-laden kiss that held a promise of passion and satisfaction.

'More champagne?'

He should just be showing her to her room, as he'd intended when he'd formed this bizarre back-up plan yesterday. But even then, as she'd stood so proudly in his office, he'd found the cocktail of icy control laced with underlying passion tempting. Too tempting. And challenging. What man could refuse such a challenge?

'No, thanks.'

Her frosty tone made it clear the ice maiden was back. He watched as she walked across the room to look down on the Thames, at the city's lights reflected in the dark water.

Ordinarily, if he'd taken a woman back to a hotel suite, he wouldn't be thinking of any kind of drink. He would be enjoying holding her, kissing her, and thinking only of satisfying their sexual needs. But this was different.

It unnerved him, but he quickly pushed the notion to the back of his mind. It was different simply because of the deal they'd struck. Never before had he spent time with a woman for any other reason than that he wanted to.

'Coffee?'

'No, thanks.' She turned to face him. 'We both know this isn't for real, and there isn't anyone here to witness anything more, so can we just say goodnight and go to bed—separately?'

He raised his brows at that last word and was rewarded with a light flush to her cheeks, giving her an air of innocence. Their eyes met and for a moment it was as if everything hung in the balance. Boldly she held his gaze.

Did she have any idea how magnificent she looked? A glacial beauty with barely concealed simmering passion.

'I'll show you to your room.'

He turned and broke the contact, but could feel her gaze following him. A sizzle of desire zipped through him and he gripped his hands into fists. If she could be so coldly in control, then so could he.

Her heels tapped rhythmically as she walked behind him, out of the vast open space of the living area and into a long corridor. He stopped outside a door, opened it, and reached in to flick on the light. 'I trust this will be comfortable for you?'

Then he looked at her face, saw a moment of hesitancy in eyes which now sparkled like rich mahogany.

'If you need anything I'll be in here.'

He pushed open the door to the master bedroom, where the lights of the city were visible for miles through large windows.

'I won't need anything,' she said, lifting her chin defiantly, and he fought hard the urge to lower his head and capture those full lips beneath his. He wanted to taste her again, to feel her mould to his body as if she were meant to be there.

'I'll see you in the morning, then,' he said, and stepped away from her—away from the temptation of her body, away from the sweet seductive scent that wrapped itself around him.

In that moment he realised he was no better than his father if he couldn't allow this woman to sleep alone. But she fired something deep within him. Something so powerful he didn't want to ignore it.

'Goodnight,' she whispered. and moved into the room, using the door to shield her glorious body from his view, apprehension clear in her eyes.

Anger simmered in his blood, mixing with unquenched desire. He was worse than his father, moving from one woman to the next. Memories from childhood, of watching an endless stream of woman enter his home, surfaced like a tidal wave. Was he now just as bad, if he couldn't walk away from Georgina?

'Goodnight.' His voice was harsh as he battled with emotions long since packed away.

Damn it all—this was a business arrangement, a means to an end. If he couldn't get out of that clause in the will legally, then he would damn well take her up on her proposition. Keeping the business was his priority. Nothing else mattered. And if Georgina had offered herself as a sacrificial lamb, so be it. Soon she would be his wife, and he had no intention of saying goodnight then.

CHAPTER THREE

GEORGINA WOKE WITH a start. Her heart thumped in her chest like a hammer as she tried to blink away the images that had haunted her sleep. Images of Santos kissing her, wanting her. Images that had heated her body as surely as if he had spent the night next to her.

She dragged in a sharp breath and looked around the room, different now the calm light of dawn was casting its glow. Her jade dress was draped over a chair, just where she'd left it, and she pulled the sheet tighter against her, feeling suddenly naked in her underwear.

Waking up in a man's bed, even if it was only the guest bed, was something she wasn't used to. She groaned at the thought of the field-day the press would have if they ever found out.

She hadn't given a thought to the morning as she'd left the party last night. Her mind had been elsewhere, thanks to Santos's charm attack.

In that moment she knew she couldn't face him. There was only one option. She had to leave now.

Could she make a quick getaway? The thought raced into her head and quickly she flung back the sheet and grabbed her dress. The silk was cool against her skin as she stepped into it and embarrassment washed over her as she thought of all those who'd know about this walk of shame.

She would be able to slip away without seeing Santos, she reassured herself, especially at this early hour.

She washed her face in the en-suite bathroom, trying hard to remove the traces of last night's make-up before applying fresh mascara and lipstick—all she'd been able to fit into her evening bag.

At the bedroom door she paused, took a deep breath, forcing her racing heart to calm before slowly opening it. Silence greeted her and she smiled, sure she was going to be able to slip away. With her bag in her hand and sandals dangling from her fingers she closed the door and padded softly along the wooden floor of the hallway, but as she entered the vast open living space the smell of strong coffee greeted her.

Her heart sank.

Someone was up.

Did Santos have a housekeeper who prepared breakfast for him? Yes, that must be it. Could she slip out without whoever it was in the kitchen noticing her? Quietly she walked across the huge room, feeling more like an intruder with every step.

'Going somewhere?'

The deep, seductive tones of Santos's voice halted her in her tracks. She turned to look at him and tried not to react to the sexy image he created in denims and a shirt. Casual suited him. But she didn't want to dwell on that now.

'Home, of course.' She kept her voice bright, as if this scenario was one she was familiar with, and met his gaze. Lifting her chin, she made every effort to appear totally indifferent to him—which was hard when he stood before her, cool and powerful, just like the man who had haunted her through her dreams last night.

'This early?' He pushed back the cuff of his shirt and looked at his watch, a small smile lingering on his lips. 'I think you have time for a coffee first. Even the most hardened shoppers aren't about *this* early on a Saturday.'

'It's not the shoppers I'm worried about,' she said with a huff of exasperation. 'Emma will be wondering where I am.'

'Precisely.'

The curt word made her blink, and despite her need to get away she walked towards him. As she did so Santos turned and headed back into the kitchen, its sleek design as contemporary as the rest of the apartment.

'How do you take your coffee?'

'This is a game to you, isn't it?' She really wasn't in the mood for pleasantries. 'We were seen leaving the party together and your housekeeper will know I've spent the night. I think that is enough, don't you?'

Santos didn't answer, and she found herself mesmerised as he poured the coffee. In her chest her heart was pounding, and a whole stream of butterflies had taken flight in her stomach.

It's not him, she told herself firmly. *It's just that you haven't been in this situation for years*. It was exactly this kind of awkward morning-after she had witnessed her mother and her lovers enduring, and exactly what she'd then gone and done herself as a naive young woman. But she'd changed, and repeating her past wasn't something she wanted to do.

'Try this.' He took her sandals and bag from her and replaced them with a steaming mug of black coffee. 'And even if my housekeeper *had* seen you—assuming she was working, that is—I would expect nothing other than her discretion.'

He smiled at her, and the butterflies in her stomach fluttered ever more wildly, but before she could respond he continued, 'At least no one will know you didn't sleep in my bed. That would really upset our plans.'

Georgina's fingers burned, and she was sure it wasn't just the mug of hot liquid in her hands. His touch, brief as it was, had jolted her with a voltage more powerful than any coffee. She took a sip—anything other than stand and look at him, fearing that if she did he would see just what an effect he was having on her.

'We left the party together. It will have to be enough.' She instilled as much courage into her voice as she could muster, which was difficult given the way her body now tingled.

Purposefully he moved past her, to place her shoes beneath a small ornamental table and drop her bag onto its glossy surface. His expression when he turned back to her was one of guarded control.

'I'm not a man to do things by half, Georgina. If I do something, I do it properly.' He stepped closer to her, the fresh scent of pine and his dark hair still slightly damp evidence that he'd recently showered.

She thought of his kiss last night at the party. The feel of his lips on hers, the way she hadn't been able to do anything other than sway towards him, and knew he was right. He didn't do anything by halves.

'I'm sure you don't, Mr Ramirez—'

'Santos,' he interrupted, his voice firm as he moved towards her.

He was coming so near she had to brace herself against the urge to move closer to him. The desire to experience his kiss just once more was almost overwhelming. She clung to her cup of coffee as if it were a lifeline.

Distance was what she needed. Distance was the safest option. She stepped back, out of the shadow of his power. She didn't know what was the matter with her—she'd never experienced this before. It was insane. Of all the men to find herself attracted to, why did it have to be *this* man? She furrowed her brow.

'If you don't use my name, who is going to believe this charade of yours?'

He raised his brow in question at her. Did he really think he could get the better of her so easily?

'You appear to be taking this far more seriously than me,' she goaded, and took another sip of her coffee before placing it on the table. Then, turning to look directly at him, she added for good measure, 'Santos.'

'You can be assured of that, *querida*.'

His lips—the ones that had set light to a trail of heady need as he'd kissed her last night—spread into a smile of the kind that made his dark eyes sparkle, full of triumph.

'I have as much to gain from this deal as you do.'

'More, if your commitment to it is anything to go by.' The words flew from her before she'd had time to think. She had to remember her goal—the sole reason she'd even approached this man in the first place. Antagonising him could put it all in jeopardy.

He didn't respond with words, but she saw his expression change. The smile still lingered, but granite hardness blazed from his eyes and he folded his arms across his chest, highlighting the breadth of his shoulders.

'Which is why I have made plans for us to go to Spain.'

Shock coursed through her body, leaving her almost gasping for air, as if she'd been plunged into a cold sea. 'Why Spain? We can stay in London. Spend the weekend here together quite easily.' She almost spluttered the last words. 'Why do we need to go to Spain?'

Santos watched as her brown eyes widened in shock and decided he preferred her with less make-up. Her soft skin looked fresh, and he fought hard against that unfamiliar urge to reach out and brush his finger against it, feel its softness.

Mentally he shook himself. The morning after was always a time to be brief—a quick goodbye had never failed him before. So why did he want to keep her here? Was it because this morning wasn't a normal morning-after? His body still fizzed with need, despite the cold shower he'd forced himself to stand under after he'd woken alone, knowing she was there, in his apartment, as untouchable as if she was the other side of the world.

'My home is in Spain, and if we are to be married I can cut through the red tape far more easily there.'

He heard her sharp intake of breath, saw her shoulders stiffen. His gaze was drawn to the way the jade silk clung to her body. She was as desirable in the morning light as she'd looked in the subdued lights of the party last night.

He wanted her more than he'd ever wanted a woman. She wasn't simpering and needy, looking for something that he couldn't give. She was strong and as in control as he was. But underneath all that he sensed a passion that would engulf him, rendering him helpless, and that was a position he would never put himself in.

He would never be as weak as his father had been.

'I still have to go home.'

She reached past him to grab her bag and sandals, her shoulder brushing his arm. He braced himself against the urge to pull her into his arms and kiss her as he had done at the party.

'A girl can't flit off for a weekend with nothing more than her Friday evening outfit.'

Her voice was light, almost lyrical. She was obviously used to loving and leaving. She also appeared used to coping in situations like this, and he'd do well to remember that. He watched as she placed her hand on the table, leaning against it as she lifted one shapely leg and slipped on a sandal. Mesmerised, he watched her fiddle with the straps, her brunette hair cascading over her shoulder, shielding her face from his view.

She straightened, taller now. His gaze locked with hers and a sizzle of something undefinable zipped between them. She blinked, long lashes breaking the connection, and bent to put on her other sandal.

'Okay,' she said softly. 'What do I need for this wedding in Spain?'

He smiled. He hadn't ever thought he would be getting married, and never in his wildest dreams had he imagined such a reluctant bride. Women usually fell over themselves to please him, and he knew if he'd asked the magic question to any one of the glamorous models he'd recently dated they would have been dragging him away.

'Your passport and birth certificate is all you need to bring. I have everything else sorted.'

'To perfection, by the sound of it. I suppose you have organised a pre-nuptial agreement?' She pushed her thick hair behind her ear and looked straight at him, her eyebrows raised in question.

Of *course* he'd arranged a pre-nuptial agreement. Any man in his position would. He'd had his legal team on it since she'd left his office on Thursday—just as they'd been finding out if it would be quicker and easier for them to marry in Spain. Her track record showed an ability to marry for financial gain and, no matter how passionately she declared sisterly love as the reason behind her proposition, he'd decided to safeguard everything.

'It would be foolish not to, *querida*.'

Her eyes sparked with burnished gold and he knew he'd hit a raw nerve. It was well known that she'd become a wealthy woman after her husband died.

'Fine.'

The word crackled between them, and her lips were firmly pressed together, as if she was holding back what she really wanted to say.

He looked at her lovely face, her lips set in a firm line of discontent, and he couldn't help himself. He reached out and brushed his fingers down her cheek. She didn't move, didn't pull away from him, just looked at him with such wide-eyed innocence he wondered if it was the same woman he'd met a few days ago.

'It will protect us both.' Her skin was so soft he wanted more. He stepped closer, the urge to kiss her stronger than anything he'd known.

'I have packing to do.'

Georgina's heart was pounding in her chest so hard she was sure he would be able to hear it. She couldn't do this. Why ever had she thought it was a good idea? Had it *really* been her only option? Offering herself to a man renowned for his ruthless business tactics.

For a moment his gaze locked with hers, the dark depths of his eyes seeming to search hers as if looking into her soul. Just when she thought she couldn't take it any more he dropped his hand and moved away from her. As he'd done a few days ago in his office he walked to the windows and stood looking out over London.

She needed to go home and think. Once she was away from him she could think of other options, but she couldn't do any of that if he was around. Just one smouldering look from his eyes made her pulse leap. She wasn't supposed to feel anything for him, but the attraction that simmered like an undercurrent waiting to snare the unsuspecting unnerved her more than anything else.

'My car will take you to your apartment and wait while you pack.'

'Wait while I pack?' She laughed. 'Have you any idea how long it takes a woman to pack for a trip abroad?' Not that she would count herself among one of those women, but she needed time alone.

'Yes.' He turned to face her. 'As a matter of fact I do—which is why you will find just about anything you need waiting for you in Spain.'

'You've thought of everything, haven't you?' She couldn't believe the calculated way he'd planned all this. From the party where they would first be seen together to the trip away to get married.

'As I said, I do things properly. I cover every eventuality. Which is why my car will wait for you.'

'I made a deal with you, Santos.' Did he actually think she was going to run away? She was made of stronger stuff than that. 'I have no intention of going back on that deal, despite the fact that you have manipulated the situation to your advantage.'

'The "situation", as you call it, will be to the advantage of both of us.'

He smiled and his eyes darkened with the promise of something she didn't want to think of.

'Of that you can be sure.'

CHAPTER FOUR

GEORGINA HAD THOUGHT the private jet was luxurious, but the villa, with its stunning sea view, was beyond anything she could have imagined. White curtains stirred in the breeze, making the sunlight dance across the marble floor. The fashionable furnishings offered every comfort possible, giving the villa the feel of a home.

She stood and looked out of the open doors, which led onto the terrace. The heat of the afternoon sun must be having an effect on her. She'd been here for several hours and still she couldn't get over the world of opulence she'd entered. But, determined that Santos shouldn't know how out of her depth she felt, she kept her awe of her new surroundings hidden.

'We'll eat out tonight.'

Santos's voice brought her thoughts back to the present as he came to stand next to her. Each time he was near, her skin sizzled and anticipation zinged down her spine, but she couldn't and wouldn't go there. This was a business deal and nothing more. She could never allow it to be more.

She dragged her gaze from the sparkling sea and turned to face him. He too had changed. He'd washed away the hours spent travelling and stood before her looking more relaxed then she'd seen him before. She couldn't help herself and allowed her gaze to linger, to take in the latent strength of his body as he walked across the room to the doors of the terrace. The commanding strength he exuded excited her and terrified her at the same time.

'Would that be to keep up the pretence of an affair?' The words slipped from her mouth with practised ease, the facetious tone one she regularly used. 'It's obvious now why we are here.'

'Is it?'

Damn him, he appeared to be laughing at her. His new, relaxed mood made him smile at her prickly demeanour. It was as if he was genuinely flirting with her, teasing her as he might one of his lovers.

'Of course it is. This area is a playground for the rich and famous, and with them come photographers and journalists, all waiting to catch the next big story. I saw them taking photos as we arrived.'

She took a deep breath and forced herself to stop talking. Allowing Santos to see how he unnerved her wasn't going to do any good at all. If he wanted to parade her around as part of the pretence then so be it.

'For a woman who dreamt up this whole idea you're very touchy about it.'

He walked out onto the terrace, where he leant his strong arms on the balustrade. Briefly she remembered how it had felt to be held in their strength, but immediately she dragged her wandering mind back. She had to keep focused. It was almost as if he knew he was distracting her. She was convinced he was using it to his advantage.

'I didn't *dream* this up.' She flung her hands wide, gesturing around them, and pushed to the back of her mind the terms he'd agreed on, hoping it would never have to go that far. 'It's you who took the idea from marriage in name only to this—this pretend love affair.'

He turned back to face her and folded his arms across his chest, the sun behind him making it difficult to read his expression. 'This is the best way.'

'Best for who?'

She realised she'd never questioned his motivation for changing things. She'd been so desperate to achieve her aims she hadn't given it a thought. Yes, she knew he wanted the business—that much Emma had told her—but why would such a wealthy and successful man, who had women falling at his feet, agree so easily to her proposition of marriage?

'It doesn't matter who it's best for. Once we are married your sister can marry Carlo and you will have got what you wanted.'

'Not forgetting what *you* want. You will inherit the business, then we can both get on with our lives. As if this had never happened.' She kept her words firm, as if she believed wholeheartedly in what she was doing. One thing she would never do was let him know her doubts.

The clinking of ice in glasses halted further conversation as drinks were brought out to them. She watched as a petite Spanish girl placed the tray on the table before she slipped away, seeming to melt into the background.

'*Exactamente, querida.*'

He turned to face her as he spoke and a shiver of apprehension slipped over her.

'It all seems too easy, Santos,' she said, realising she'd used his name without having to force herself. 'I can't believe a man like you would agree to my deal so easily. There must be something more in it for you.'

He moved away from the balustrade and came close to her. Too close. Her first reaction was to step back, but she stood her ground and met his gaze head-on, despite the pounding of her heart and the race of her pulse. Something in his expression had changed. He looked more intense, his eyes darker. She couldn't help but look into them and momentarily floundered.

'Yes, there is, *querida*.'

He stepped closer and the air seemed alive with something she'd never experienced before.

'And that is?' She feigned bravado, her words short and sharp.

'I want what we agreed in my office. A wife.'

He was serious, and from the resolute set of his mouth she knew he wasn't going to change his mind any time soon. 'We don't need to make this marriage any more difficult to get out of than need be,' she said

'I have no intention of *getting out* of it, Georgina. I want a real wife—not someone joined to me just because we signed the same bit of paper.'

His gaze dropped from her eyes and lingered on her lips and she realised she was biting her bottom lip. The tension of waiting to hear what he really wanted was too much. As was his proximity. Her stomach fluttered wildly and she had to concentrate hard just to breathe.

'But why me?' She moved backwards, but still the sizzle was there. She could feel it with every pore of her skin. *He's just trying to throw you off balance*, she assured herself, and asked again. 'Why me, Santos? Why now?'

'Because you're the only woman who's asked me to marry them at a time when I need to be married.'

When I need to be married.

Those words rang inside her head like a cathedral choir. He didn't want to be married either, and she clung to the hope that she could persuade him later that separation was the best option.

Images of being with Santos, of spending days and nights with him, filled her mind. She became dizzy at the thought of what the nights would entail. Why did he want her in that way when he could have any one of the glamorous women who always seemed to be in his life?

Santos watched as an array of emotions flashed across her beautiful face. She might well have asked him to marry her, but he could see the idea of a real marriage unsettled her as much as it did him. Marriage was something he'd never wanted to enter into. He hated that he was being forced to marry by his father's ridiculous clause in his will. As a child he'd witnessed the destructive side of marriage—a side he knew lurked beneath every claim of love.

Love. He knew it didn't exist. It was a false and misleading emotion that could destroy any man, woman or child. It was open for exploitation. Never would he allow any woman close enough to manipulate him. Marrying Georgina was a necessity, nothing more.

'Lucky I asked when I did,' she said, and flashed a smile at him. But sadness clouded her eyes.

Was she thinking of her first husband? Had she loved him? Had he been manipulated just as easily? *Fool,* he told himself, fighting back irrational emotions that were completely alien to him. *Don't even go there.*

'Lucky for who, *querida*?' He couldn't resist the urge to provoke her, wanting to see those soft brown eyes spark with passionate fire, as they had done the very first time he'd seen her in his office.

She raised her brows at him. 'For you. I could have just encouraged Emma and Carlo to slip off and get married without anyone knowing. So I suppose you have the most to lose, Santos, and you have the most at stake.'

His name sounded hard on her lips, fierce. He wanted to go over to her and kiss them until they softened, until every last drop of restraint disappeared. Instead he focused his mind, because if one thing was true it was the fact that he *did* have the most to lose.

But he'd never admit that.

'We both have things at stake, Georgina.' Impatience crept into his voice. 'So I have had a mutually beneficial agreement drawn up.'

'Ah, the pre-nup.' She picked up her drink, ice clinking, and took a sip, all the while maintaining eye contact with him. 'I'll sign whatever is needed. I made that clear when I first put the proposition to you.'

'In that case, now would be a good time to do it.'

He saw the colour drain from her face, watched as she took a deep breath and met his gaze.

'Okay.'

That one word shook with fierce determination.

'We can finalise the formalities of our arrangement so that we can enjoy a relaxed evening out.' His business mind took over, insisting he secure everything before going any further with this deal—because a deal was all it was. One struck for the mutual benefit of both parties.

A flicker of guilt flashed into his mind. A moment ago she'd looked vulnerable, outside her comfort zone, but now she was as dignified and collected as she could be. Was she trying to throw him off balance in a bid to secure more for herself out of the marriage?

'Let's just get it done, Santos.' Her shoulders straightened and the spark of fire flared in her eyes, leaving him in no doubt that she meant every word.

He nodded his approval and admired her undaunted tone. 'The agreement is on my desk.'

He led the way to his study. For the first time in his life he was anxious about the outcome of a deal. Normally he would be in total control, able to steer deals his way, manoeuvring people like pieces on a chessboard.

But not with Georgina.

It wasn't her rigid sense of purpose or her defiance that left him second-guessing where their conversations would lead, but the woman herself. The soft curves of her delicious body, the passion in her eyes in those rare unguarded moments, always left him feeling distracted.

He wanted her.

But she was unlike any woman he'd wanted before. He sensed she was different, sensed that he had to play it cool. He knew she was like a proud lioness, knew that she would show her strength, her courage, but if she needed to she'd turn and flee, leaving him in the dust. And if she did that all would be lost. She was, after all, his last hope—his legal team had made that clear—but, like a card player, he'd keep his hand close to his chest and certainly wouldn't be revealing the full extent of the will just yet…not when he was still trying to get his head around it himself.

He clenched his hands and drew in a deep breath. Damn Carlo. His rush to marry had forced him to contemplate things he never would have entertained before.

He gestured to a chair on one side of his desk, taking in the graceful way she sat and noting the guarded expression on her face. He had to handle this as he would with any deal—ruthlessly. It was the only way. Otherwise he risked being weakened by her smile or, worse, by the undercurrent of something passionate that always seemed to surround them. How much of that was an act on her part he wasn't sure, but he had to fight hard against the way his body responded to her.

'My legal team have drawn up an agreement in Spanish and English. I think it will be beneficial to us both.' He kept his voice controlled as he took his seat opposite her, then he turned the document round and slid it across the desk towards her.

Their eyes met and a simmer of tension passed between them. She lowered her lashes and with slender fingers drew the document closer to her. He watched as she read the conditions, certain she'd be happy with his generous terms.

'It looks very comprehensive.'

She glanced up, but he wasn't sure if he was relieved or not to see a teasing smile on her lips.

'You obviously feel the need to protect yourself from my scheming ways.'

'It protects us both.'

He tried unsuccessfully to keep the irritation from his voice. Did she *have* to remind him of her past right at this moment? Was she proud of all the men she'd dated within weeks of her husband passing away? He pushed to the back of his mind all he'd learnt about her after that first visit to his office.

She raised her brows at him suggestively. Damn, was the woman deliberately trying to provoke him?

He stood and walked round the desk and leant down, one hand flat on the hard polished surface, bracing his arm. With pen in hand he pointed at the contract. 'As my wife you will be entitled to a substantial allowance to do with as you please.' Her perfume invaded his senses and he realised his mistake in coming close. 'Any children the marriage produces I will stand by and support, regardless of the outcome of our marriage.'

At least he'd touched on the subject of children. It was hard to believe that he, a man who'd never wanted to be married and certainly hadn't wanted to father a child, now sought both. Or at least was being forced to.

'Children?'

There was no doubting the shock in her voice. He looked down into her eyes, bright and wide. 'Yes. Children.'

He watched her slender throat as she swallowed and guilt sliced at him. He should tell her that a child might well become essential to secure the business, but something kept him silent. He wasn't sure if it was the fear of spooking her or the still raw anger at his father for creating such a clause. He had mentioned he wanted a *real* wife—surely that left her in no doubt.

He hoped he'd never have to go that far. It went against everything he believed in. As a *mistake* himself, he did not want to bring a child into the world unless he could give it love and security. The latter wouldn't be a problem, but love…?

'Do you want children?'

Her hesitant question made him clench his jaw and he saw her gaze dart to the movement, then quickly back to his eyes.

Georgina had asked the question lightly, despite the way her stomach had flipped over and was now churning. Did he really anticipate children? From a short-term marriage contract? She hoped not. Having a child was the one thing she'd never wanted to do. It was simply out of the question.

She looked down at the contract, the words blurring on the page as she fought back memories of her childhood. A childhood that had left her scarred and certain she didn't ever want to be a mother.

'As I said, I have covered all eventualities—to protect both of us.'

She swallowed hard and looked again up into his eyes. Their dark magnetic depths almost made her lose her nerve. For one tiny second she imagined a child with eyes the same colour, but quashed the image before it could manifest itself into anything bigger.

She had to have breathing space. His closeness, the fresh scent of his aftershave and the heat of his body so close to hers, was undoing her last remnants of self-control. She needed space and she needed it now.

'You have covered everything concisely, just as I would have expected from you.' She picked up the pen and with a flowing movement of her wrist signed the contract. The pen dropped to the desk as she pushed back the chair and moved away from him—away from the power he had over her every time he came close. 'There. All signed.'

'You don't have any questions?' He looked startled by her bravado and stood straight, towering over her, leaving her no option but to stand and face him.

'Just one.'

'And that is?'

'When are we going to finalise this deal and get married?'

That isn't the question, her mind screamed as she watched a sexy smile spread across his lips. *You should have asked when you can call Emma*, she scolded herself. She wanted to tell her sister that she could start making plans for her own wedding.

'Tuesday.'

'What?' All the air seemed to have left her lungs, as

if she'd run into a brick wall, and her heart was pounding madly. 'But that is only three days away.'

'Is there a problem with that?' His voice resonated with control and his expression hardened in challenge, the smile of moments before gone.

'No…no,' she stammered, hating herself for doing so. 'I just hadn't expected it to be so soon.'

'I see no reason to delay.'

His eyes hardened and his voice was firm as he spoke and she knew deep down that he was right. The sooner they were married the better. But Tuesday felt all too soon. She hardly knew him. *You don't need to*, a nagging voice inside her chided.

'I'll need to get something to wear. I'm sure you don't want your bride turning up in jeans.' She tried at humour, but her voice sounded brisk even to her ears.

He looked at his watch. 'That wouldn't be the image I was planning—which is why I've arranged for outfits to be brought here this afternoon. Select whichever one you want, and also something suitable for this evening.'

The velvet-edged strength of his voice and sexy accent caused her to drag in a ragged breath.

'What exactly *is* this evening?' In a bid to quell the nauseous tremor in her stomach she lifted her chin, dropped her shoulders and met his gaze.

'Our engagement.'

The words were curt and she watched as he walked back around to his side of the desk. He picked up the pen, pulled the papers towards him and signed next to her signature on the contract before looking back up at her.

'I fully intend for us to be seen out this evening as if we are a couple madly in love.'

'It's only Emma who needs to think we actually *want* to get married. It doesn't matter to me what anyone else thinks—not now.' She couldn't believe he wanted to put on a public engagement.

'I don't want doubt in anyone's mind,' he said as he sat back and looked up at her. 'Least of all people I've known for many years. I want them to think that we are in love.'

'There will be people you *know* there tonight? Not family, surely?'

It was all getting too much. Everything was happening so fast—much faster than she'd ever planned. She was getting deeper and deeper all the time into something she obviously hadn't given enough thought to.

'*Sí*, my cousin.'

Amusement shone from his eyes. Was he enjoying her discomfort?

'Other than that, just friends—but they will talk. I want the right things said.'

Further conversation was halted as the maid Georgina had seen earlier knocked on the door. Spanish words flowed melodiously between her and Santos, and Georgina felt strangely excluded. Her grasp of the language was basic to say the least.

'I shall leave you now to select your wedding gown. Señora Santana is well known in Spain for her gowns.' He turned his attention back to her, the smile that the maid had been treated to still lingering on his lips.

She felt a nervous panic at the thought of being left alone, hardly able to communicate with his staff, let alone whoever was here with wedding outfits. Santos laughed. A soft throaty chuckle that was maddeningly sexy.

'Don't panic. I shall be in here. I have plenty of work to do.'

'I'm not panicking,' she flung at him, and smiled at the maid, who was waiting to show her where to go. How did he always manage to know what she was thinking?

'I'll wait for you on the balcony at seven,' he said as she left the room.

She stopped on the threshold and turned to look at him. His tall frame dominated the study so that he seemed almost dangerous. And he was, if the way she reacted to him was anything to go by.

Georgina was taken to yet another bedroom, as big and airy as the one she'd been shown to on arrival. The only difference was the rail of white and cream silk almost mockingly awaiting her approval. One glance at the dresses and Georgina knew that most of them weren't suitable.

'*Buenas tardes, señora.*' An immaculately dressed woman in her forties all but glided across the marble floor. 'A little too romantic maybe?' Her accent was heavy and she stroked the dresses lovingly and smiled at Georgina.

'I have already been married….' Georgina began, resenting the need to explain anything, but Señora Santana put up her hand as if to tell her to stop.

'Not a problem. Señor Ramirez has explained,' she said, and walked behind the rail of dresses to another which Georgina hadn't noticed.

Just what had Santos explained? Curiosity piqued, she followed and drew in a breath of awe. These dresses were beautiful. Bold colours of red, green and midnight-blue had been added to frills or even completely forming a bodice.

Georgina couldn't help but smile. These were more like it. A sweet, innocent bride was not the image she was going for. She trailed her fingers over the silk and chiffon. But one dress in particular caught her attention. She took the dress from the rail and held it against her. It was perfect. It was everything, and more, that she could want this dress to be.

'*Perfecto.*' Señora Santana smiled and urged Georgina to try it on.

Caught up in the moment, she relished the feel of silk and chiffon against her skin and looked at her image in the mirror. The dress fitted perfectly. As if it had been made for her. She slipped her foot into a dainty strappy sandal, feeling more and more like Cinderella every moment.

'You will need a veil.'

'No,' Georgina replied quickly, and glanced in the mirror at the other lady. 'No veil,' she said more gently, and smiled. She hadn't had a veil for her first wedding—hadn't even had a dress—so she saw no need to go over the top now. Especially as it was, once more, a marriage of convenience.

Señora Santana shrugged. 'Ah, I have the perfect alternative. You will see. But now we choose a dress for dinner. No?'

No was just what Georgina wanted to say. She'd gone along with the wedding dress, knowing it was part of the whole plan and necessary. Photos would almost certainly end up in the glossy magazines, whether she wanted them there or not. But a dress for this evening wasn't necessary. At least not one of this quality.

'No, the wedding dress is enough.'

The woman's eyes widened. 'But Señor Ramirez insisted. You *must* choose one.'

Finally Señora Santana's insistence had worn Georgina down and she'd selected a classic black dress, which now lay on her bed. The hours had just disappeared whilst she was trying dresses on, leaving very little time before she was to meet Santos. Now, after a quick shower, she dried her hair and applied make-up.

Why was she feeling nervous about seeing Santos again? She looked at her watch. Five minutes to seven. He would be waiting on the terrace very soon. She looked again at the dress, feeling almost like a sacrificial lamb.

But wasn't that exactly what she was?

For her sister's happiness she'd once again taken on a role she didn't want. Marrying Richard had been to put Emma through school and a roof over their heads. It had been his suggestion, and even to this day she couldn't believe a man had done that for her. She'd been on tenterhooks during all the three years they were married, just waiting for him to leave her. But she'd never expected him to leave her the way he had. As a widow. She'd known he was ill—but not that ill.

With a heavy heart she picked up the dress, stepped into it. For a moment the zip eluded her and it took several minutes of contortions to pull it up. Flustered by her efforts, she slipped on the new pair of shoes insisted upon by Señora Santana and left the bedroom, her heels sounding loud on the marble.

CHAPTER FIVE

SANTOS WAS LOOKING out at the sea, dressed in a dark suit, as she approached the balcony. When he turned and his gaze met hers her breath caught in her throat. It wasn't right that a man could be so sexy. The cloth of his suit had been cut with precision, emphasising his broad shoulders and strong thighs to perfection.

She swallowed hard, desperate to calm her racing heartbeat. If she carried on like this there wouldn't be any need for pretence. Her attraction to him was becoming stronger, and if he turned on the charm as he had at the party she'd be lost. Worse still, if he kissed her again she didn't think she'd be able to resist him.

'You look beautiful,' he said, his voice deep, with a husky edge to it. 'Exactly what I had in mind.'

Well, if that didn't serve as a reminder that it was all an act, then nothing would.

'I'm glad it meets with your approval,' she said tartly and, desperate to hide her confusion, walked past him to the table, selecting a drink from those prepared. Anger fizzed in her veins at the thought of the way he made her feel: light-headed and soft one minute, then short and sharp the next. In a bid to rein in her rising and very mixed emotions she all but downed her drink in one go.

'Steady, *querida*.' He smiled. A mocking smile. As if he knew her turmoil. 'That drink is pretty potent.'

She looked at the almost empty glass. The remains of the liquid looked more like a soft drink, but its effect on her head was already clear. Whatever was she trying to do to herself? She put the glass down and turned to look at him, holding her hair back as the sea breeze toyed with it just as he was toying with her.

'If you are ready shall we go?'

He didn't wait for her to answer, but placed his hand in the small of her back, its heat scorching through the silk of her dress, and all but propelled her towards the door. Outside, a sleek, gleaming sports car waited, fiery red. Exactly what she'd imagined him driving.

'Suits you,' she said in a cavalier tone, and dropped down into the low seat as he stood by the open door.

He raised his brows and smiled at her. '*Gracias*.'

When Santos climbed in beside her she became all too aware of just how close she was to him. His tanned fingers pulled the gearstick backwards as the car growled into life. She couldn't help but notice that the space beneath the steering wheel seemed almost too compact for his powerful thighs.

A small but insistent fire sparked to life deep inside her as she watched him drive. Each move he made sent a shiver of awareness over her and she bit down hard on her lip against the new wave of emotions that assailed her. She couldn't be falling for him—she *couldn't*.

'Is it far?' Nerves made her voice quiver as she finally acknowledged the attraction she felt for him, and he glanced across at her before returning his attention to the road ahead.

'No, but arriving in style will attract the attention we need.'

'Attention?' Her mind was scrambled as she looked at his profile. The shadow of stubble only added to the sexy appeal he emanated.

'How else is the world going to know we are engaged?' He glanced across at her again, his gaze meeting hers briefly before returning to the task of driving. 'This is what you wanted. Puerto Banus is a renowned favourite of the rich and famous, and with them come the press photographers, hungry for gossip.'

Now she understood his insistence on dressing for dinner. This was Act Two. The next part of their public courtship, played out to perfection. It was time to retreat behind her public persona.

'And tonight, *querida*, we shall give them something to gossip about.'

His voice was laden with promise and as the fire rose higher inside her she looked away.

The car growled into the small harbour town and Georgina couldn't help but take it all in. Cars as sleek and powerful as Santos's lined the narrow streets, parked outside global designer shops. Yachts that looked more like floating palaces were moored all around the harbour, many with lights glinting and parties in full swing on board.

This was most definitely a playground for the wealthy.

Santos parked the car, expertly manoeuvring it into a space in front of one of the bigger yachts. He switched off the engine and silence seemed to cloak them. The leather seat crunched as he turned to face her.

'You look absolutely stunning tonight.' He reached up and pushed her hair back from her face and she trembled.

She didn't say anything. She couldn't. All she could do was look into the mesmerising depths of his eyes.

'You are playing your part well—so well even I'm convinced.'

His voice was a husky whisper and she wished he wouldn't slide his fingers through her hair like that.

'Convinced of what?' She forced the words out, alarmed at the throaty sound of her voice.

'The attraction between us…'

He moved a little closer and she wondered if he was going to kiss her. She wanted him to, but knew it would be her undoing. Then, before she even had a chance to think, his lips claimed hers. Try as she might she couldn't stop her eyes from closing, couldn't help reaching up to touch his cheek, feeling the slight stubble against her fingertips. She was attracted to him, despite all she'd promised herself, and he must never know. That would be to show her weakness. Give him all the power. She'd seen it before.

She pulled back a little from him, her lips still very close to his, and opened her eyes. 'I'm a brilliant actress,' she whispered as her fingers smoothed once more across his face.

The sound that came from him resembled a growl as his hand caught and held hers. 'Don't take your role too far, *querida*. I might just go past the need to act.'

For a moment she sat transfixed by the tension that hung between them. The promised threat of his words was not lost on her. Did her really want her? Did he find himself struggling against the same raw need she was fighting right now?

'It's showtime, Georgina.' His words were firm and sharp as he pulled away from her and got out of the car.

She watched him walk around the front of it, relaxed but masterful. Obviously she didn't have the same effect on him—didn't scramble his emotions until he couldn't think straight.

Okay, showtime it is, she thought as she got out of the

car and walked with him towards the busy street lined with restaurants. She could do this—even if it meant putting on the biggest show of her life.

Suddenly a man's shouts caught her attention and a waiter from one restaurant came out to greet him, hugging Santos and then stepping back to cast an enquiring look her way.

'Georgina, this is my cousin Raul—owner of this restaurant and at our bidding for this evening.'

She felt suddenly shy beneath the man's gaze. He took her hand and with the same charm Santos possessed kissed it. 'I can see why my cousin is so entranced.'

To her horror she blushed, but managed to smile back at him. 'What more could a girl ask for?' She raised her brows, made her voice light and melodious, even a little flirty.

Raul laughed and after a brief look of shock Santos did too. Then he smiled at Georgina, a dangerous light in his eyes.

'Raul, do you have the table I requested?'

'*Sí,*' Raul replied, and continued in Spanish.

Santos put his arm around her shoulders, pulling her close as he followed his cousin to their table. It was private, and candles fluttered in the evening breeze. The sea could be heard lapping gently onto the shore close by.

It was perfectly romantic.

The whole meal was. Each course was divine and all the while Santos exuded what she was fast becoming aware was his lethal charm. She smiled, played her part all through dinner, but reality was beginning to blur. She sipped her wine and looked out at the sea, where the setting sun cast an orange glow across the rippling surface.

'Georgie?'

Her attention swung back to Santos when she heard her

name on his lips. His voice sounded hoarse, as if he was choked with emotion. Oh, he was good at this, she thought, and smiled at him. He'd never used her pet name before.

'Will you marry me?'

'What?' she gasped as he slid a small velvet box across the table. *Calm down. It's probably for his cousin's benefit.*

'Will you make me the happiest man alive and marry me?'

His dark eyes were watching her intently. When she looked into them she thought she saw the same desire she'd seen at the party, the same simmering passion. Just as she'd thought she'd seen it earlier, when they were in the car. But that couldn't be, could it?

She reached for the box, aware of the role she had to play, but he caught her hand in his. The heat of his touch was almost too much.

'Marry me?'

'Yes.' Her whole body quivered, but she couldn't lower her gaze, couldn't break that tenuous connection. 'Yes, I'll marry you.'

Slowly he let her hand go, opened the box and pulled out a glittering diamond ring. As he slid it onto her finger the candlelight made it sparkle, bringing it to life. He lifted her hand to his lips, his gaze holding hers captive, and kissed her fingers.

This was what it would really feel like, she thought as she looked into his dark eyes. This was be the closest she'd ever come to having a real proposal.

Applause erupted around them, making her jump. She hadn't realised they were being watched, and neither had Santos. Even he looked taken aback. She laughed, unable to help herself, and the tension of the moment slipped away as the other diners returned their attention to their meals.

'Let's go,' he said in a throaty growl, sounding as if he really couldn't wait to get her home. Something indefinable skittered over her, making her tummy somersault and her breath tighten in her chest.

Don't do this to yourself. You are just a means to an end. He doesn't really want you.

It was dark as they walked back along the street. Yachts were lit up, giving everything a magical appeal. The warm breeze on her skin felt wonderful, but not as wonderful as Santos's arm about her waist, pulling her against his magnificent body. She savoured the moment, stored it for later. The champagne she'd drunk was making it easier to enjoy being with him like this and easier to let go of her usual anxiety. This wonderful feeling was going to have to last her a lifetime.

By the car Santos stopped. Instinctively she looked up at him, then couldn't help herself as she reached up and kissed his lips. His response was gentle at first, setting her body alight. The fire was fuelled further by his hands sliding down her back, pulling her so very close to him. Whatever it was that had simmered between them at the party was now well and truly alight. As her hips pressed against his aroused body she knew he wanted her. Was it so wrong to give in to it? To enjoy it for what it was? A passing attraction.

'Santos,' she murmured against his lips.

It was all the encouragement he needed and he deepened the kiss, plunging his tongue into her mouth as she sighed in pleasure.

Need rocketed through her body and she almost became incapable of thought as he stepped closer, forcing her back against the side of his car, pressing hard against her and stoking the fire deep within her body. Unleashing an insatiable need for him.

His hand slid down her side, over her hip and down to her bottom. He pulled her hard against him and raw desire tore through her, leaving her gasping against his lips as her arms clung around his neck. It was mind-blowing. She'd never known anything like it.

A flash lit up the world for a second—or so it seemed to Georgina. But in that second she regained her breath, and the control she'd so very nearly lost. She turned her face to the opportunist photographer, knowing he was just what she needed to bring her feet firmly back to the ground.

Beside her Santos spoke in Spanish, his voice thick and hoarse as the photographer snapped another photo. Quickly Santos put some distance between them and opened the car door for her, but she didn't miss the raw desire in his eyes.

Once they were inside she asked, 'What did you tell him?'

'That we'd just got engaged and needed private time.' His voice was husky and heavily accented.

Of course he'd say that. But she couldn't help feeling humiliated. His kiss—which had been part of the act, the charade—had nearly been her undoing. She'd wanted more…wanted him to take her home. More than anything she'd wanted him to take her to his bed. But that could never happen.

Never.

To allow him to know how much her feelings towards him had changed would be the worst possible scenario. With that in mind she retreated to her room as soon as they arrived back at his villa.

The next morning Georgina used the excuse of it being Sunday and stayed in her room. Eventually she ventured out, hoping the quietness of the villa meant Santos was ensconced in his study.

As she strolled through the living area movement in the pool caught her eye. Santos was powering through the water, his strokes effortless. She shouldn't be watching but couldn't help herself, almost unaware of each step towards the pool she took. The afternoon sun shone brightly and she put on her sunglasses, watching as his muscles flexed.

Abruptly he stopped and looked at her, his dark eyes gleaming with amusement. 'Are you coming in?'

The husky depths of his voice made her stomach flutter and she was glad of the sunglasses she could hide behind. 'I'll give it a miss,' she said as she sat down on the edge of a sun lounger, even more drawn to him.

'Pity,' he replied, and swam over to her. His hair was flat against his head and rivulets of water ran down his face. 'It's very relaxing.'

Hardly. The thought of being in the water with him made her pulse race, and inwardly she cursed the attraction she felt for him. It was making things complicated.

'Maybe a walk along the beach?'

'That would be nice,' she said, and stood up, aware that at any moment he would haul his bronzed body from the water. And she wasn't ready for that. 'I'll go and change.'

Not trusting herself to look back at him, she hurried to her room and changed into a cool dress and flat sandals. Regaining her composure, she returned to the terrace and waited.

She knew when he was there as if her body was completely tuned in to his. She turned to face him and that spark of attraction zipped instantly between them.

'Shall we?'

He took her hand and for a moment their eyes met,

his darkening instantly. She remembered his touch last night, his kiss, and could hardly draw breath.

Right now, with his hand holding hers she felt safe. Cherished.

As if he could read her thoughts he held her hand just a little tighter. She smiled a genuine smile, one she couldn't hold back, as he stepped closer and brushed his lips over hers.

Everything around her ceased to exist. It was just the two of them. No deal—nothing. When he pulled back she looked up into his eyes. Was this what she'd been searching for? This strange warm feeling of contentment?

'We won't get very far like this,' she teased lightly, her heart almost melting as he laughed softly.

'*Sí*, you are right. We will walk.'

Sand, warm from the afternoon sun, poured into her sandals, but she didn't care. She just wanted to savour this moment. Because this was what it must be like, that glowing feeling of a new relationship. The first tender stirrings of love. Was it even possible?

'You're smiling,' he said as he pulled her to a stop, his hand not relinquishing its hold on hers. 'For the first time since we met you look happy.'

'I am.' And she meant it. Right now all she wanted was to be herself, to bask in the warmth of this new sensation. Santos made her feel things she'd never thought possible, and knowing those feelings wouldn't last for ever she wanted to relax and enjoy them. 'What about you?'

'In the company of a woman as beautiful as you, how could I not be happy?'

She searched his eyes, looking for a hint of mockery, but found only a heart-rending tenderness. He stroked his fingers down her cheek, lifting her chin as he bent and lightly kissed her lips.

Her heart pounded erratically and a tingle of excitement raced around her. Light-headed and almost giddy, she kissed him back, tentatively at first. This wasn't the needy kiss of last night—this was giving and caressing. It was loving.

She pulled back from him a little, shyness making her look up from under her lashes as heat infused her cheeks. 'You don't have to say and do these things—not now, anyway.'

'What I say is true.'

His voice was husky and raw as he brushed her hair back from her face, sending waves of delicious sensation all over her.

'And I only do what I want.'

It was as if a bond was forming with each gentle caress of his hands and each soft word. He was pulling her towards him. This man was so far removed from the compelling man she'd first felt a spark of attraction for she was lost for words.

Without another word he pulled her against him, holding her so close she could hear his heart thumping as wildly as hers. Was he aware of what was happening? Did he also feel as if he was wading out to sea, getting deeper and deeper, unable to turn back to the safety of shore?

The next morning Santos planned to work, but all he wanted was to be with Georgina. It was as if magic had been in the air last night on the beach and had weaved around them, bringing them closer in a way he'd never been with a woman before.

Was it because she still hadn't shared his bed? Was that one fact making him delusional? Like a man lost in the desert?

A bit of distance, that was what they needed, he decided, and for the best part of the day he shut himself in his study. He tortured himself when he heard her in the pool, but it was more than desire that raced around his blood. Something new, something undefinable, now simmered there too.

Finally, as the sun was setting, he could stand it no longer and went in search of the woman who would tomorrow be his wife. She was curled on the sofa, her phone in her hand. She looked up at him as he stood in front of her.

'I can't get Emma on the phone.' Her words were rushed.

Guilt shot through him, he'd completely forgotten her need to phone her sister.

'I sent a text instead.'

He didn't know how to respond to the obvious anxiety in her voice. Worrying about siblings was not something he'd ever done. Distraction was what she needed, he decided. 'Would you care to join me for a walk?'

'Another walk? Tonight?' She put her phone on a nearby table and smiled at him, the same warm smile she'd given him the night before. 'It's supposed to be bad luck for the bride to see the groom on the eve of her wedding.'

'I won't tell if you don't,' he teased, and held out his hand to her. She hesitated, then laughed softly. It was such a sexy sound he had to brace himself against the onslaught of thudding desire which rushed over him.

'In that case, how can I refuse?' She seemed different, as if all pretence had been abandoned, and he knew this was the real Georgina. The fiery, demanding woman who had burst into his office last week no longer existed.

The sea was calmer than he'd ever known it, with the waves hardly making any sound. They walked along the sand hand in hand, as they had done the previous afternoon. The sky was dark and the stars were shining brightly as he stopped and turned to her.

'I've enjoyed your company,' he said awkwardly. 'It's hard to believe it's only been a few days since we arrived.'

Georgina looked up at him. Was it possible he felt it too? He was so different now, so relaxed, and she knew she was in danger of falling in love with him.

'Don't say any more,' she whispered, putting her finger on his lips. She didn't want him to give her hope if he didn't mean it.

He kissed her fingers and before she knew how she was in his arms, her body pressed close to his. Fire tore through her as she kissed him, giving way to all the new emotions she was battling with. She wanted him with a fierceness that shocked her.

He deepened the kiss, his arms pressing her close against him, leaving her in no doubt that she needed to stop things now. She pulled back from him, her heart racing, and her breathing fast.

'I can't, Santos.'

'Can't what?' His voice was hoarse and he tried to kiss her again.

'This,' she said, moving back from him. 'We shouldn't even be seeing one another tonight. It's bad luck.'

CHAPTER SIX

SANTOS'S PULSE POUNDED in his head and a fire coursed through his veins which had little to do with the punishing early-morning run he'd just completed. After yet another night of trying to douse his need for Georgina he'd given up and, despite it being the morning of his wedding, had gone out to find some kind of release. He wasn't sure how much more he could take.

How could one woman drive him to such distraction?

Refusing to explore the answer to that question, he returned to his villa. As he did so he heard female voices and knew that Señora Santana had arrived, along with the others, to do the bridal hair and make-up. He clenched his hands into fists, fighting hard against the urge to go to Georgina's room, send everyone out and continue what she'd started last night—because start it she most definitely had.

Patience, he reminded himself, and headed for a cold shower instead. His run had not had the desired effect. Heady lust still throbbed through his veins and he knew of only one antidote for that—other than taking Georgina to his bed right now. *Work*. Once he'd showered he would shut himself in his office and work until lunchtime, when he would escort Georgina to the beach to become his wife.

An hour later he admitted it was impossible. The figures blurred before him and all he could think about was that kiss last night. At first so innocent and tender, then passion had taken over. Santos realised he'd been so consumed by need he'd behaved like a teenager, raging hormones taking control of his senses, rendering him completely under her spell.

Just as his father had been with Carlo's mother.

That thought alone had the sobering effect he needed on his body. He could never allow himself to be at the mercy of a woman—wanting her so much that nothing else mattered. Not even his inheritance. He'd never wanted a serious relationship, and certainly didn't want to get married, but his father's interfering had changed that.

In a bid to divert his mind he turned to his laptop, scanning the business pages and the headlines from Spain and England before looking at the celebrity gossip columns. Sure enough, just as he'd expected, he and Georgina were featured leaving the party together. Speculation as to what would happen next had filled the columns for the last two days.

At least now nobody would think him grasping enough to marry purely for financial gain. That sort of reputation wouldn't go down well when making business deals in the future. But if his business rivals thought he had a human side, one touched by love—whatever that was—they would be less guarded with him, giving him the edge he always sought.

He looked up at the clock on the wall. Eleven-thirty. Almost time to seal the hardest deal of his life. He turned off the laptop, put away his papers and headed back to his room to put on his suit.

As he fixed his cufflinks he looked in the mirror. Was he doing the right thing? He thought of the clause in the will, the need for an heir, and knew in that moment he should have told Georgina exactly what might be expected of her unless his legal team could find another way out. So why hadn't he? Because he didn't seriously think it would come to that when he was paying to find a solution. But then he hadn't thought he'd ever have to marry either.

A knock at the door drew his attention and he strode over to open it, knowing he was to be given the message that she was ready. It was time to make Georgina his wife. Guilt shot through him. She didn't know exactly what she'd signed up for. He had to tell her as soon as they were alone. Tell her that his mention of children in the prenuptial agreement might prove vital in the deal she'd come up with. Even *he* wasn't that harsh. Despite everything, he still clung to the hope that it wouldn't be necessary.

She was waiting for him on the terrace, but nothing could have prepared him for that moment if he'd spent several years organising it, instead of several days.

Georgina looked amazing.

Cream chiffon and silk encased her slender figure, but the slit in the floor-length dress drew his eye to her leg as she moved towards him. Her dark hair had been pulled back into a chignon and lace was attached to it, giving her a very Spanish air. The bodice of her dress clung to her breasts lovingly and on the single strap diamonds sparkled.

'I trust this meets your requirements?'

Her chin lifted defiantly, and her voice was as sharp as a razor, but her eyes still blazed with the same desire he'd seen in them last night. Gone was the woman he'd held in his arms as the stars sparkled above them.

'Every bride should look stunning on her wedding

day,' he said firmly, admiring the confidence that radiated from her. 'And you do.'

He fought to stop his mind envisaging removing the gown later as he truly made her his. Because if the attraction that existed between them—the one they had both been trying to deny—finally got the better of them when they were alone, there would be no doubt about consummating their marriage.

'You look very handsome too,' she said, a small blush creeping across her cheeks, her words softer.

'I'm pleased you didn't choose one of those fussy, frilly gowns I saw being brought in.' He tried to lighten the mood with small talk, but each step she took towards him showcased her slender legs and it was having a powerful effect on him. 'Such a daring dress was made for you.'

'Having been married before, I didn't think the usual fairytale image was appropriate.' She followed his lead and kept her voice light.

'It is far better than what you wore the first time,' he said slowly, his gaze holding hers. 'A business suit at a registry office? Hardly the stuff of fairytales.'

'You know that?' Her beautiful dark eyes widened slightly and she drew in a sharp breath.

'I always research my business deals, Georgina, and this one is no exception.' His words sounded firmer than he'd intended as he remembered exactly why they were doing this. The effort of not reaching for her, taking her in his arms and kissing her as he had last night, was almost too much. 'Ready?'

She looked at him for a moment, her brown eyes cool and emotionless, then she swallowed hard, giving away the fact that she wasn't as composed as she wanted him to think.

'I'm ready.' Still her voice was hard, full of determination.

He took her hand and led her from the terrace, down the steps towards the beach, where his cousin and a friend waited to witness their marriage. He glanced at her, smiling at her continued air of defiance.

Pride unexpectedly swelled in his chest as he realised just what was about to happen. He was about to take this gorgeous woman as his wife—a woman any man would be proud to be seen with. She was clever, witty, and incredibly sexy. Her hand in his was small and he clutched it tighter, enjoying the warmth of her.

Georgina's step almost faltered, and it was nothing to do with the grains of sand sliding through her sandals as she made her way across the beach. It was everything to do with the proud and arrogant man at her side.

His hand was warm as it held hers and she risked a quick look at him. He looked as if he'd stepped from her long-ago abandoned dream of a happy-ever-after. He was exactly the image of the man she'd used to dream of marrying: tall, dark, and devastatingly handsome. But this man was also dangerous. The way he could send her senses into overdrive meant she had to guard herself well or risk being hurt.

The waves rolled onto the sand before rushing back to sea and Georgina wished she could slip away with them. Doubts… Surely they were natural for a bride, but they clouded her mind, making her homesick. She wanted to see Emma, to tell her what was happening. This morning she'd nearly called her, but as she'd looked at her sister's number she'd known she didn't have enough strength to conceal the truth.

She wished she had someone here she knew. Someone for *her*. Someone who could reassure her she was doing the right thing.

When Santos stopped, not far from Raul and two others, she knew it was too late.

'I'm sorry there wasn't time to find one of your friends to witness this.'

Santos spoke softly next to her ear, almost making her jump and dragging her from her melancholy. It was as if he knew her thoughts.

She smiled brightly at him—maybe a little too brightly. 'It might have given the game away if you'd started flying my friends out here.'

'If you're sure?'

'I'm sure,' she replied quickly, injecting as much bravado into her voice as possible. 'Let's just get this over and done with.'

He looked shocked, but time for any further discussion was lost as the minister greeted them.

Everything seemed to spin. The minister's words, first in English, then Spanish, blended with the rush of the waves. Santos continued to hold her hand tightly and the heat of his body beside her was matched only by the sun.

She couldn't think—couldn't even grasp the concept of the words that were being said. When she'd walked into Santos's office last week she hadn't envisaged this— a beach ceremony with a man she was finding ever harder to resist. A man who wanted to be married to her about as much as she wanted to be to him.

'Georgie?'

She looked slowly up at him, remembering the need to act like a real bride, and smiled. He smiled back. A smile that reached into the dark depths of his eyes, melting her from the inside out.

He took her hands in his and spoke in Spanish to her.

She had no idea what he was saying, what he was doing. Everything seemed unreal. Then he slid a gold ring on her finger, repeating the words in English, and she realised he was doing exactly what she should be. Acting.

Panic raced through her. She didn't have a ring for him. Should she have got one? A polite cough at her side caught her attention and Raul handed her a ring, his smile full of charm. She smiled and turned back to Santos, slid the ring onto his finger and repeated the words that bound them legally in a marriage neither wanted.

Moments later Santos covered her lips with his, almost knocking the air from her as his arms wrapped around her, pulling her closer. She should resist, but sparks took off inside her like New Year's Eve fireworks and she wound her arms about his neck. It was as if the desire of last night still simmered.

Just as suddenly as the kiss had begun it ended, and Santos pulled away from her, but he kept her hand in his as he thanked Raul, his friend and the minster. Spanish flowed around her and all she could do was stand and wait, trying to come to terms with what she'd done.

It's for Emma. Just as it was last time.

'Now it is time for us.' Santos returned his attention back to her, his dark eyes sparking with fire.

'Us?' she asked as she watched the three people who'd witnessed her marriage walk back across the beach.

'*Sí.*' He dropped a kiss lightly on her nose and she blinked in shock at the affectionate gesture. 'We have to have at least a few days for our honeymoon before we return to London.'

Honeymoon.

Had he gone mad?

'Is that really necessary?' She couldn't believe he was serious. 'We're married now. You've got your business.

Can't we just go back and tell Emma and Carlo they can get married?'

'This was your idea, Georgina. You wanted to make it look as real as possible.' He frowned and looked down at her, his hand still clasping hers.

'I only wanted our names on a marriage certificate. I didn't want all this *acting*.' She should never have hoped to change things so late in the day. Not when she was dealing with a man like Santos.

His dark eyes narrowed in suspicion. 'You wanted authenticity and you've damn well got it.'

He let go of her hand and stepped back from her, then turned and walked back to the villa. She watched him go, just as she'd watched her father go all those years ago.

What was she doing? She couldn't stay on the beach—an abandoned bride for all to see. Propelled into action, she kicked off her sandals, picked them up and marched after him. They'd been married for only a matter of minutes and were already arguing. Surely that would make him see they needed to go their separate ways?

'Okay,' she said as she caught up with him, injecting as much ferocity as she could into her voice. 'We'll have the honeymoon. But once Emma and Carlo get married this farce ends.'

'Farce?'

He stopped and turned to face her. The fury in his face served only to increase her need to keep what she really felt for him concealed.

Without warning he pulled her into his arms, his lips claiming hers in a demanding and hungry kiss, weakening her body so that she could barely stand. She wanted to respond, wanted to take the pleasure his lips promised, but instead she reminded herself it wasn't real. None of it was. At least not for him.

His hands pressed her ever closer to him, until she had no doubt that although the marriage wasn't real his desire for her was. Her lips parted and his tongue plundered her mouth, entwining with hers in an erotic dance, making her sigh with pleasure.

Heaven help her, she wanted more. She wanted this man in a way she'd never wanted a man before.

He pulled back from her, his breathing deep and ragged. 'Now, deny that, Mrs Ramirez. Deny that you want me. Deny what your body tells me.'

'This wasn't supposed to happen.' Her lips were bruised and her body trembled with unquenched desire as she looked into his eyes, seeing sparks of passion within their depths.

'Come,' he demanded as he took her hand, and the gentleness of yesterday was gone.

Was he about to drag her to his room, take her to his bed? Excitement fizzed in her veins, only to be replaced by disappointment as he walked straight through the villa and out to his car.

'Where are we going?'

He opened the door of the car for her and she got in, hampered by the silk and chiffon of her dress. Mesmerised, she watched his hands expertly gather the silk skirt and bundle it into the car, his fingers brushing against her bare leg where the gown so daringly parted. She shivered as their eyes met. Their gazes remained locked; his hand rested on her leg.

'To my yacht.'

His voice was deep and incredibly seductive. Her heart jolted and her pulse raced as his fingers trailed over her thigh, moving teasingly higher.

'For our honeymoon.'

The smouldering flames she saw in his eyes should

have been warning enough, but she didn't want to listen to sense any more. This man wanted her, desired her, and she wanted him too. All sensible reasoning slipped away as he bent and kissed her thigh, where his fingers had made a blazing trail.

'Santos.' She placed her hands either side of his face, forcing him to look up at her. 'Please don't. At least not here.'

He smiled and stretched up to press his lips to hers, breathing Spanish words against them. She had no idea what he said and neither did she care. She watched, anticipation throbbing in her blood, as he shut the car door and strode around the front to the driver's side. He looked at her as the engine growled to life, his gaze so hot it seemed to melt the chiffon from her body and dissolve the silk of her skirt. And when those dark and dangerous eyes met hers she knew it was already too late. She'd lost. His expert charm and arrogant confidence had won.

She was as good as his.

She sat silently contemplating what had just happened between them as Santos drove. The car sped along the coast road, but she didn't doubt his ability to handle it. The sea glistened in the afternoon sun and she realised that very soon they'd be alone out there.

Tyres screeched as he came to an abrupt halt next to what was probably the biggest yacht in the harbour. She wasn't sure if she felt relieved or disappointed that they weren't going to be alone after all. A yacht this size must have at least a dozen crew members.

As they boarded he fired off rapid instructions in Spanish and everything seemed to come to life around them. A maid stepped forward, offering a glass of champagne, and Georgina took it, grateful to have something to hold other than Santos's hand.

She looked at him and he raised his glass to her. 'To my beautiful wife.'

His gaze openly devoured her and her body tingled.

'To my handsome husband,' she flirted.

Just one sip of champagne was making her braver than she really was. She had to play the game well, so she smiled as he smiled. But her words weren't lies. He was more handsome than she could ever have dreamed of, standing on deck in his designer suit, glass of champagne in hand, passion for her sparking in his eyes. He was everything and more from her abandoned dream of the perfect man.

'As we sail we shall have our wedding breakfast.'

He sipped his champagne and she watched him swallow, mesmerised by the movement of his throat. Food was the last thing she wanted right now, but maybe it would bring her back to her senses, dull the thud of desire in her veins and enable her to think rationally.

Whilst they'd been talking the yacht had slipped away from the harbour and was now sailing past the long stone wall and out into the sea. The small but affluent town of Puerto Banus looked picturesque, nestled below the looming mountains, and Georgina was transfixed by the view.

'So beautiful,' she whispered, unable to drag her eyes from it.

'Beautiful indeed.' Santos's voice was firm and strong as he stood next to her. 'But it is outshone by the beauty of my bride.'

Georgina took another sip of champagne—anything to calm her nerves—and then turned to face him. 'Surely we don't need to keep up the pretence here?'

His hand reached out, his fingers lifting her chin so that she had no option but to look at him. Her legs became unsteady and she wondered if it wasn't more to do with the man next to her than the motion of the yacht.

'Tonight I ask only one thing of you, Georgina.'

Her heart accelerated and pounded in her chest like a drum. Her gaze locked with his, held there by only the smallest touch of his fingers to her chin. Her breathing deepened and she wondered if she'd be able to stand for much longer so close to him.

'And that is…?' She maintained control of her voice, but control of her body was much harder. Heat was building low down in her stomach, spreading slowly and re-lighting the fire that had so nearly consumed her last night.

'No pretence. Not tonight, at least.'

Santos saw her eyes widen, watched as the soft brown of her irises turned darker until they were as black as the night sky. Her full lips, the ones that had kissed him almost into oblivion last night, parted and he fought hard against the urge to crush them beneath his.

'Not even a little bit?' She smiled up at him, and a hint of mischief danced in her eyes.

She was still hiding herself from him.

'No.' He lifted her chin a little higher and brushed his lips against hers, feeling her body tremble as it so nearly touched his. She smelt good, her perfume sweet and light. 'No pretence at all, Georgie.'

He liked calling her that. It made her seem more real—warmer, somehow. Like the woman he'd glimpsed last night. And tonight he was determined to find her again. It was *that* woman he wanted—the woman who'd filled his dreams and every waking moment since.

He took the glass from her hand and without taking his eyes from hers dropped it onto a nearby seat. The yacht lurched as they headed out to sea, pitching her against him, and instinctively he wrapped his arms around her, keeping her close.

'You can let me go now,' she said firmly, her breath feathering against his chin as she looked up at him. 'I wouldn't want you to think I'm throwing myself at you.'

He laughed and let her go. 'I wouldn't ever think that of you.'

She was so vibrant, so beautiful, and she was his wife.

As he faced her he saw shyness spread over her face— an emotion he would never have associated with the demanding woman who'd all but barged into his office last week.

Her fingers brushed his and his pulse raced in anticipation, just as it had been doing every time she came near him. It was almost torture, wanting a woman and not being able to have her. But tonight would be different. Tonight she would be his.

He watched as she walked away from him, the sandals she'd struggled with on the beach long since abandoned. The wind whipped at her dress, lifting the silk around her, allowing him more than a glimpse of long slender legs as she moved inside the yacht.

Pushing back the carnal thoughts that filled his mind, he followed her—and almost stopped in his stride when he saw the sadness on her face as she stood and looked out of the window. Was she thinking of her sister? Missing her?

'I'm sorry there wasn't anyone at the wedding for you.' Uneasy guilt compelled him to say it again, despite her earlier assurances.

She turned and looked at him, blinking her lashes rapidly over her eyes. 'It's not as if it was a real wedding—if it was I'd have insisted on Emma being there.'

She shrugged and looked back out at the retreating coast-line. 'Besides, you only had your cousin.'

'Raul *is* my family.'

'I've never heard Emma or Carlo mention him before.' She rubbed her hands on her arms as if cold.

'He's my mother's brother's son, so not a blood rela-tion to Carlo.' His clipped words caught her attention.

'You make it sound as if having a stepmother and half-brother is a bad thing.'

This was the first window into his life he'd allowed her to see through, and it made him feel vulnerable, but he was strangely compelled to talk and continued.

'My father and I were happy enough after my mother left, but when she died in an accident a few years later my father went to pieces. It was as if he'd been waiting for her to come back to him.'

He'd never told anyone that before. Talking of his childhood was something he just didn't do. But memories rushed back at him now like a sea wind, keen and sharp.

'I'm sorry,' she said softly, touching his arm. 'It hurts when a parent leaves. As a child you feel...' She paused and his heart constricted. 'Responsible, somehow.'

He looked down at her upturned face, at her soft skin glowing in the late afternoon sun, her eyes full of genu-ine concern. When was the last time anyone had been concerned about him? He wanted to talk to her, share his memories with her. After all she knew something of his pain—his research on her had proved that.

'My father had a second youth—dating women as if they were going out of fashion. So when he met the woman who would later be my stepmother it was a re-lief. He settled down again. I just hadn't expected to be excluded from the family when Carlo was born.'

She frowned slightly but said nothing, her steady gaze encouraging him to talk.

'As time went by Carlo became the centre of everything and I stood on the outside, looking in. I refused to compete for my father's attention. When I left university I began to take over the running of the investment business and my father spent more and more time with his *new* family.'

'But surely they loved you?'

He could see pity in her eyes, the image he'd painted for her, and anger surfaced. He did not need her pity. Just as he hadn't needed his father's love as a boy.

'*Love*, Georgina? What is *that*?'

His words were sharper than he'd wanted. He sensed her draw back from him, both physically and emotionally, and was thankful when she didn't say anything else.

'You're cold,' he said when she shivered. 'We will go inside and eat.'

As far as he was concerned the discussion was now closed.

He led her inside and even he was stunned at the intimacy of the small feast that had been prepared for them. The large table was set at one end, just for two, candles glowed and rose petals were scattered across the cream tablecloth. He heard her stifled gasp of shock and smiled.

'Your staff have excelled themselves,' she said softly as she came to stand beside him. 'It looks divine.'

The intimacy only increased once he was seated at the table with her, the soft glow of candlelight casting her face into partial shadow. Her shoulders were bare apart from the one strap of the dress. They looked creamy, soft, and he wanted to touch her skin, to kiss it, taste it.

Food was the last thing he wanted.

* * *

Determined not to be put off by Santos's sudden change of subject, and desperate to keep her traitorous body under control, Georgina spoke. 'I can remember my father walking away late one summer's evening. It was dark and hot, and later there was such a storm I worried all night about him. It sounds like it was tough for you too after your mother died.'

He'd almost opened up to her—almost let her in.

His face hardened and she knew she'd touched on a nerve.

'It was. But I'm not going to talk about such things now.'

He offered her some of the delicacies on the table, his fingers brushing hers, causing her to look up into his eyes.

'There are far better things to talk of on our wedding day.'

Our wedding day.

The words hung in the air between them as his dark eyes held hers. She should say something—anything. But she couldn't. The intensity of the attraction sparking between them was too much.

'You're not eating.'

He glanced quickly at her untouched plate and her pulse-rate leapt as once again his gaze held hers.

'It's looks delicious, but—'

'You're just not hungry?' He cut across her words, then took her hand, his own tanned one covering hers easily, sending shock waves of heat up her arm, and she was glad he'd forgotten the talk of his family.

'No,' she answered boldly, and wondered what he would say if she told him just what she *did* want right now. Would he laugh at her if she told him that all she could think of was kissing him, feeling his arms tight around her? She just couldn't fight the attraction any longer.

'So what *does* my sweet bride want?' He raised her fingers to his lips, dropping lingering kisses to each finger, and all the while he watched her, his eyes darkening with desire. 'Remember,' he teased, his voice deep and heavily accented. 'No pretence—not tonight.'

'I want…' She paused and smiled coyly at him as he waited. 'You.'

Shock laced with excitement fizzed in her veins as he raised his brows, slowly and suggestively. Once more he kissed her fingers, each time lingering longer, until she couldn't stand the anticipation any more.

He stood up from the table, keeping a tight hold on her hand, and pulled her up against him, holding her close.

Music began to drift around the room, reminding her that they were far from alone, that the crew and staff were lingering in the background to do his bidding. The disappointment she felt at not being totally alone with him shocked her. She wanted what they'd shared over the last few days.

'It is a tradition, is it not, for the bride and groom to dance together?'

He was so close now she could smell fresh pine mixed with the musky scent of pure male. It was intoxicating.

'In England it is, yes.' Her voice was little more than a husky whisper.

'Then we dance.'

He walked away from the table, guiding her to the middle of the room as the gentle rhythm of the music continued. When he held her close once more her knees threatened to give way, so intense was the attraction between them. It was an attraction that had been stamped out several times already, but Georgina knew this time it was going to be different—because this time she wanted him with a fever that engulfed her whole body. He was her husband now, and despite trying not to she had feelings for him.

This was how a bride *should* feel, and she pushed back memories of the clinical registry office service when she'd married Richard. It might only be for this one night, but she knew she had to live for the moment—had to surrender herself to it completely. This could be her one chance of sampling such heady romance.

As those thoughts flickered to life in her mind Santos kissed her—a soft, lingering kiss that held the promise of passion, one that awakened every nerve in her body. She deepened the kiss, closing her eyes against the onslaught of pleasure which crashed over her like waves onto the beach as she pressed close against him, feeling the evidence of his desire.

Breaking the kiss, he began to move her slowly around the room to the sound of the music. How could a dance be so erotic, so loaded with sexual tension and the promise of passion? The intensity of it was so much that she longed to give in and rest her head against his shoulder, close her eyes.

No pretence...not tonight.

His deep, husky words replayed in her mind.

Should she allow herself to taste what it might be like to love a man? To feel what it would be like to be loved back? Santos certainly seemed to be playing the part of devoted lover today. She didn't think for one moment it wasn't part of the charade they had created, but right now, as his arms held her close, the idea of happy-ever-after seemed tangibly close.

She laid her cheek against his shoulder, a soft sigh

escaping her as she closed her eyes. He tensed, and she knew he hadn't been able to abandon the idea of pretence completely. He was as on edge as she was, which made her a little less vulnerable—because together they could abandon the carefully constructed façades they each lived behind.

His arms tightened around her body, pulling her closer to him, and heat raced through her. As he pressed his lips into her hair she closed her eyes again, the sensation too much, and focused all her attention on the music instead of the feel of his strong body.

As she moved with him she realised the movement of the yacht had changed and glanced at the shoreline.

'Have we stopped?' Her words were husky. She'd never heard her voice like that.

'*Sí, querida.*'

He brushed his lips over hers as she looked up at him, sending another flurry of tingles skittering over her.

'We are to anchor here tonight. The crew and staff are leaving. They will be back in the morning.'

'So we will be completely alone out here?'

'Very much so.'

He stroked a hand down her face and she fought the urge to turn and kiss it.

'Does that worry you, *querida*?'

It should worry her, but it didn't. She wanted to be with him like this, to feel his body against hers, to taste his kisses. How could she pretend otherwise?

She searched the dark depths of his eyes, dropping her gaze to his lips briefly before looking back into his eyes. 'Should I be worried?' A flirty edge had slipped back into her voice as she struggled to keep her emotions under control and stay behind the safety of the barrier she'd erected long ago.

His voice was deep and incredibly sexy as he rubbed the pad of his thumb over her lips, making her lose those last doubts.

'Only if you don't want me to sweep you up into my arms and carry you to the bedroom.'

CHAPTER SEVEN

RIGHT NOW THAT was all Georgina wanted. It was all she could think about. It was as if the gently lapping sea beyond the yacht and the warm breeze had conspired against her. The luxury of everything was feeding the romantic dream she'd long ago abandoned.

But for tonight at least she could live it. Tonight she *would* live it—would allow herself to taste what she'd never thought possible.

'What more could a girl ask for from her groom?'

Her heart thumped in her chest and her breathing deepened, so that she had to drag every breath in, but still she couldn't quite let go of the bravado she always hid behind even as her body yearned for his.

In one swift movement he swept her feet from the floor to hold her firmly in his arms. The silk of her skirt fell apart at the slit and the heat of his fingers on her thigh scorched her skin, bringing a blush to her cheeks.

He swung round so that the tiny spotlights in the yacht's ceiling blurred behind him as she watched his face. It was set firm, as if his jaw was clenched.

'Then we will waste no more time.'

The depth of his voice, so sensual, laden with intent, sent a ripple of awareness cascading over her.

She felt every step he took as he marched through

the living area. A harsh Spanish curse left his lips as he reached the curving stairs which she guessed led to the bedrooms. Only vaguely aware of her surroundings, she remained focused on his face, but when he looked down at her the intensity of desire burning in his dark eyes made her smile.

He didn't smile back. His face remained set in firm lines. 'Damn stairs,' he growled, and turned his body slightly as he carried her upwards.

She reached up and touched his face, a small sense of triumph shooting through her as he dragged in a ragged breath. His skin was smooth, despite the darkness hinting at fresh stubble growth as her fingers slid down to his neck.

'You can put me down.' Her voice was barely above a whisper.

'Not until I have you where I want you.'

The strength of his words made her shiver with excitement.

As he reached the top of the stairs she looked around her and saw open double doors through which was the most magnificent bedroom she'd ever seen. Briefly she took in the dark mahogany furnishings and the big bed, its cream covers scattered with pink rose petals, as Santos walked briskly towards it.

Gently he placed her on the bed, and she leant back on her arms as he stood like a magnificent bullfighter at the side. She trembled as he looked down at her, his eyes as dark as the depths of the ocean.

Nervousness suddenly washed over her. It had been a long time since she'd been in a situation like this, with a man openly desiring her, his intentions clear. Would he be expecting the practised lover that society thought she was? The temptress she willingly portrayed herself to be?

'And this is exactly where I want you, *querida*.'

As the slow, purposeful words came huskily from his lips she watched him undo his tie and drop it to the floor, his jacket soon following.

Hungry for him, she let her gaze devour the strength in his arms as his white shirt pulled tight across his biceps. She bit her lip as he undid the top buttons, exposing dark chest hair and tanned skin. All the while he watched her with such intensity she knew she would be powerless to resist him.

Keeping her gaze locked with his, she reached up to her chignon, but something in his expression stilled her hand. The smouldering passion she saw in his eyes sent a dizzying current through her.

'Don't.'

His voice was harsh, and the arrogance that surrounded him maddened and excited her at the same time.

'But…' she whispered as he stepped closer to the bed, towering over her, dominating the very air she breathed.

'I've wanted to free your hair all day.'

He knelt on the bed beside her, his weight making her sway towards him as the mattress dipped. Within seconds he'd released the pins that secured her hair and she felt it slide over her shoulders.

'I've wanted to see it around your shoulders in all its glory.'

She closed her eyes against the sensation of his body so close to her, inhaling the intoxicating male scent that was uniquely Santos. When his lips pressed briefly against her shoulder she gasped softly in pleasure.

She opened her eyes and turned to face him, momentarily shocked at how close he was. His handsome face was only inches from hers. 'Santos…' she whispered as he kissed her cheek, her forehead, her nose, stoking the ever growing heat deep inside her.

'I want you, Georgie,' he husked out between each kiss. 'I want to make you mine.'

'I want that too.' And she did. Nothing else seemed to matter now except the two of them.

He silenced her with a long, lingering kiss that drew every ounce of reservation from her body, replacing it with unadulterated need. A small sound of pleasure escaped her lips as he broke the kiss, only to be smothered as his lips claimed hers in another greedy kiss that rocked her to the core.

Santos shook with need as he deepened the kiss. Never before had he felt as if he was on the edge of control with a woman—but then never before had a woman played so hard to get.

Her hand touched the side of his face, her palm pressing his cheek as she kissed him back, need for need, her tongue teasing his. He broke free of the kiss and looked at her full lips, already bruised from his kisses, then to her eyes, darker than he'd ever seen them.

She moved back from him, further up the bed, and a hot stab of lust grabbed him as her slender legs were exposed yet again. Teasing and testing him. He took hold of her foot and slowly undid one sandal, pulling it from her before tossing it to the floor.

She smiled and for a moment he thought he saw shyness in her eyes, but then it was gone as she lifted her other foot. He took it, and again slowly removed the sandal, but this time he didn't let go of her ankle. Unable to help himself, he smoothed his palm up her leg, past her knee, until it slid underneath the silk of her dress. A dress he desperately wanted to remove from her.

She closed her eyes and dropped her head back against the bed, a look of total abandon on her face as his hand slid higher. The warmth of her skin was almost too much for him. *Patience*, he urged himself. This was a night to take it slowly. This was a woman to savour.

He reluctantly moved his hand down her thigh, past her knee and back to her shapely ankle.

'How does a man get his wife out of her wedding gown?'

His voice was uneven and ragged. He was using every last bit of control just to stop himself from taking her right now.

'At the back.'

The words were a tremulous whisper, serving only to excite him further. He was used to his lovers being bold, but he liked this air of innocence she'd adopted.

She sat forward, waiting for him to unzip the gown. Sitting back on his heels, he steadied himself as he reached behind her and undid a clasp, then slid the zip down her back. His anticipation almost boiled over with every breath she breathed against his naked chest. Her scent invaded his senses and he dragged in a deep breath, tasting her.

At last the bodice of the gown sagged around her and he moved back, catching a glimpse of creamy soft breasts as it slipped lower. Part of him wanted to rip the gown from her, but a more disciplined part of him wanted to savour the moment, to make it special for both of them. It was, after all, their wedding night.

He kissed her, pushing her back against the pillows as his tongue delved deeper into her mouth. She tasted of champagne and his senses fizzed like a shaken bottle. Her arms wound their way around his neck, pulling him down to her, pressing against her.

He spread his hand over her bare shoulder, enjoying the feel of her skin, then slowly slid it downwards—until he met the resistance of the gown's bodice and wished he *had* ripped it from her.

She moved beneath him, thrusting her breasts upwards, inviting him to touch them—an invitation he had no trouble in accepting. His hand pushed aside the bodice, cupping her breast, his thumb and finger rubbing over the hardened nipple.

'Oh, Santos,' she whispered against his lips as her body arched even more. Need rocked through him.

Words failed him as he kissed down her throat, over her collarbone and down to her breast, finally taking her nipple in his mouth as her fingers ploughed through his hair. But still it wasn't enough. He wanted more—much more.

He pulled himself away from her, smiling at the disappointment on her face as he did so. 'This has to go.' He took hold of the bodice of her gown and pulled. Her breasts were slowly revealed, and then, almost erotically, her flat stomach and her beautifully shaped hips were laid bare to his hungry gaze. 'So beautiful, *mi esposa*.'

She smiled at him. And again that shyness he'd glimpsed earlier was in her face as she lay partially naked before him.

He kissed her stomach, revelling in his mastery as her body arched towards him again, begging him for more even if the words didn't come from her lips. Still lower his kisses went, until he found the silk of her panties. She bucked wildly beneath him then, almost undoing the control he was desperately hanging on to.

He looked up at her, at her dark hair spread about her on the pillow in sexy disarray, eyes closed as she enjoyed his touch. No sign of shyness now.

Agilely he rose from the bed, amused at the expression on her face as she looked at him, questions in her gorgeous eyes. As he pulled the wedding gown down she lifted her bottom, enabling him to pull it away in one go, leaving her dressed in only cream silk panties.

She looked divine.

And she was his.

'It's not very fair if you remain dressed, is it?' Her smile was coy and teasing as she looked up at him, completely at ease with her near nakedness. An accomplished temptress.

He undid the remainder of his shirt buttons with deft fingers and pulled it from his body. Her gaze roved hungrily over his body before finally meeting his eyes, and passion charged around him as his heart thundered like a herd of wild horses.

The air was electrified and he pulled off the remainder of his clothes without breaking eye contact. Her eyes were sending him a secret message of desire and need. How had he ever thought this woman cold?

Georgina couldn't help but look at him. Arrogantly naked before her, confidence in every move he made. She knew he'd achieved his aim. He'd made her desire him, want him completely. Every nerve in her body ached for his touch and being naked to his gaze excited her. Never before had she wanted a man as she wanted Santos.

Shyness took over once more, but she tried to act as if being naked in front of a man—a man as naked as she was, who so obviously desired her—was something she was more than used to. She watched as he sat back on the bed, his legs astride hers, rendering movement almost impossible. His aroused body was magnificent, and so very tantalisingly close to her, intensifying the rush of need, of raw desire she'd never known before.

He hooked a finger in the top of her panties, his gaze locking with hers. 'These too.'

Before she could say or do anything he'd pulled them down. The silk slid from her effortlessly and, in what she could only guess was a well-practised manoeuvre, he pulled them from her legs and threw them to the floor without moving from her at all.

She was exposed, naked and vulnerable, but for the first time in her life she didn't care. All she cared about right at this moment was satisfying the burning need she had for this man.

Her husband.

Her body ached for the fulfilment of his body. She wanted him in a way she'd never dreamt possible, and sparks of excitement at the prospect of being his shot round her.

He bent low over her and kissed her stomach before moving down further, his breath warm, sending fire gushing through her. She closed her eyes to the pleasure of his exploration. When she thought she couldn't take it any more his kisses moved back up her stomach to her breasts. In turn he kissed each hardened nipple. He pushed first one knee between her legs, then the other and, giving herself up to an instinct as old as time itself, she opened her legs, wanting to feel him deep inside her, desperate to be at one with him.

Her fingers gripped his shoulders as his erection nudged her moistness. He lowered himself onto her, kissing her as his body shook with the effort of holding back. She felt his heated hardness teasing her, and then, just when she thought she couldn't take one more second of it, he thrust deep inside her. She gasped at the pleasure of his possession, her fingers gripping ever tighter to his shoulders as she moved with him. Her legs wrapped around him, pulling him deeper into her, and he groaned in Spanish and thrust harder, deeper.

Their rhythm increased until she couldn't help but cry out in joy. A new and exciting sensation washed over her and she opened her eyes to look out of the sloping windows above the bed, feeling as if she too were flying among the stars that now sparkled above her in the night sky.

Santos's body shook and he cried out before burying his head in her hair, his body pressing hers into the bed. She wrapped her arms tightly around his back, keeping him there, wanting to feel him deep within her.

Finally her heart-rate began to slow and her breathing returned to normal. Santos lifted his head and looked into her eyes. 'Now you're truly my wife, Georgie.'

She didn't know what to say—what to do, even—so she just smiled back, her body still too sluggish with the aftermath of passion.

Santos rolled off and away from her and the cool evening air shocked her naked body, making her shiver. He reached down, grabbed a throw from the bottom of the bed, pulled it up over them and, to her total amazement, pulled her close.

She hadn't expected this. She'd thought he would disappear to the bathroom and come back partially clothed, ready to move on from what they'd just shared. Was this relaxed closeness part of his idea of no pretence? Was this the real man he didn't want the world to see?

'I should have asked this sooner,' he said, his voice sounding strangely unsure, and she wondered what was coming next. 'But we didn't use any contraception.'

'It's okay,' she whispered softly, and trailed her fingers down his arm, feeling a thrill of excitement when he groaned and pulled her close against him. Her mind quickly raced, wondering where her handbag was. Thankfully she'd put her contraceptive pills in there when she'd hurriedly packed for Spain. Not that she'd thought she'd actually need their protection. 'It's sorted.'

He stiffened slightly. 'Even so, I should have at least asked, but—'

'Don't worry. There won't be any repercussion from tonight. Just sleep.' She kissed him lingeringly on the lips, feeling the tension slip from him. Finding herself pregnant was not an option she relished, and she was certain he'd feel the same. 'Relax, Santos, try and sleep.'

He kissed her, pulling her close against his nakedness, stirring slumbering desire again. 'How can I sleep with you naked next to me?'

'At least for a while,' she teased as he kissed her again, his hands smoothing over her back.

She closed her eyes against the rising need for him, determined to play it cool. He must never know just how much she wanted him at this moment.

As he slept his breathing became deeper and steadier, and in the dim light of the bedroom she could see his naked back. Her fingers were desperate to touch him again, to create a trail over his tanned skin. The temptation became too much and she moved, but as soon as she did his relaxed hold on her tightened and he mumbled something in Spanish. It was enough to stop her.

Instead she lay and looked up at the night sky through the sloping windows just above the bed. The motion of the yacht was soothing and finally she relaxed, after what felt like days of being on edge, waiting for Santos to pull out of their agreement. They were married. The deal was well and truly sealed.

Tomorrow she'd call Emma, tell her to make plans for her own wedding. She smiled, remembering the morning she'd first met Santos. His arrogance and undeniable air of authority had almost made her turn and run from his office. Never in her wildest dreams had she thought that the man she'd proposed to as part of a business deal would end up being the first man she'd ever wanted—*really* wanted. The first man to show her just how good loving could be. The first man she could love, if only she let herself.

He didn't love her and had gone to extreme lengths to tell her he couldn't love anyone. He might have discarded pretence for the night, but would tomorrow be different?

Santos murmured again, pulling her against him and kissing her hair, sending a rush of heat through her body. Firmly she closed her eyes against the new wave of desire that was washing over her—because surely tomorrow it would be different.

Tomorrow she had to focus on Emma, on making sure Santos kept his side of the deal.

Santos woke in the early hours of dawn, his body heavy and relaxed in a way he'd never felt before. Georgina's scent lingered on the pillow next to him, reawakening the desire that had coursed like an overflowing river through him last night.

From the other side of the room he heard movement and he propped himself up on his elbow. With amusement he watched as Georgina, sexily naked, appeared to be looking for something to put on. He took in her slender waist, shapely hips and long legs as she stood, her back to him, looking around the room.

'*Buenos dias, mi esposa.*' *My wife*—that was something he'd never thought he'd call a woman.

She turned to face him and despite her nakedness looked as in control as she always did. For him, last night had changed something, softened the way he felt about her, but apparently it was not the same for her. She looked as if finding herself naked in a man's room was perfectly normal. A situation she was well used to.

'Morning,' she replied huskily, a smile playing about her kissable lips. 'I was looking for something to put on.'

'Your bag is in the wardrobe, but you will also find everything else you need in there too.'

Transfixed, he watched as she walked across the room, the swell of her breasts causing the blood to pound in his veins. If she didn't put something on very quickly she'd find herself back in his bed.

'Very convenient.'

The hint of sarcasm in her words was not lost on him. Keeping an array of women's clothes in his villa or on his yacht was not something he'd done before—but then catering for a future wife was not something he'd had to do either.

'I was merely trying to think of your convenience, *querida.*'

She opened the door of the wardrobe, assessed the contents, then opted for a cream silk dressing gown. She slipped it on and pulled it tight around her, knotting the belt at her stomach. The garment should have doused the fire now raging in his body, but it didn't. The outline of her body, still clearly visible, was more teasing than seeing her naked.

'Come here.' His voice was gruff and husky as desire pumped through him.

Instantly she looked shy, a blush creeping over her face, and he wondered which was the act. The bravado he saw more often or the innocent shyness she now displayed.

Slowly she walked towards the bed, her eyes darkening, remaining locked with his. He reached towards her, grabbed her hand and pulled her down to the bed.

'Santos!' she gasped in shock. 'What are you doing?'

'I would have thought that was obvious, *querida*.' As she lay beside him on the bed, her breathing faster, her breasts rising and falling in the most erotic way, he pulled the belt undone and pushed aside the silk, exposing her delicious body. 'I'm going to make love to my wife.'

Those words lit a raging fire inside him.

Unable to analyse those feelings now, he silenced her with a kiss so hard and deep he almost couldn't breathe. His need for her was far greater than last night—as if now he'd tasted her he needed more, like some kind of addict. Her hands explored his body, pushing aside the sheet and touching him until he couldn't stand it any longer. Urgently he pushed her back against the bed, covering her body with his as he thrust hard and deep within her delicious warmth.

It was as if his whole world rocked as he climaxed, relishing the feeling of being deep inside her. She cried out, her body arching towards him as she too found release. As his heartrate slowed and his mind regained the ability to think he realised he'd done the one thing he'd never done before. Early-morning sex. It gave women the wrong message. Made them think he wanted more.

But Georgina was already his wife. What more could she want from him?

He lay back, exhausted and exhilarated at the same time, his breathing and heart-rate finally returning to normal, and contemplated what had happened. Because something had changed, but he just couldn't understand what.

* * *

'I'll just go and shower.' More vulnerable than ever, Georgina wanted to put a little distance between herself and this man's magnetism.

'Don't be too long, *querida*.' He smiled at her, sending her senses into a spin as her heart flipped over.

Instead of answering him, she slipped from the bed with a bold teasing smile, grabbed her abandoned dressing gown and headed for the bathroom.

How on earth was she going to cope with today after what they'd shared last night? Would his rule of no pretence continue into the first day of their married life, or would he return to being the arrogant and controlling man she knew he was?

The hot water of the shower did little to ease her worries and she knew she had to talk to Emma. Just to hear her sister's voice would reaffirm why she'd married Santos.

With a towel wrapped round her body she emerged from the bathroom to find the bedroom empty. Quickly she reached into the wardrobe for her bag and pulled out her phone to see Emma had sent her a message.

OMG Georgie! You and Santos!

As she read the text from her sister she could almost hear her voice, the laughter in it—relief, even—and quickly she called Emma.

'Georgie!' Emma's excited voice was so vibrant it was as if it was on loudspeaker.

'Emma, I *so* wish you could be here, but...' Georgina swallowed. The first lie was about to leave her lips. 'We just had to get away and be alone.'

'You're really happy?'

'Do you think I'd jet off to Spain if not? After all that I've been through?' Thoughts of Richard mixed with the lies she was telling, the web of deceit she was spinning. *It's for Emma*, she reassured herself.

'Then I'm happy for you—but can you do one thing for me?'

'Anything for you, Emma.' That at least was true.

'Don't come back just yet. Carlo and I... Well, we're going to arrange our wedding, and if Santos finds out he's sure to put a stop to it. He's so against us getting married.'

Georgina swallowed hard. She should tell Emma. Instead she lightened her voice. 'We're enjoying our time together.' Was that a lie? she wondered as her body warmed at the memory of last night—her wedding night. 'Do you really think we're going to rush back to London?'

As she ended the call she let out a big sigh—relief that her sister and Carlo were now actually able to plan their wedding. She wished she'd been able to tell Emma that Santos was now her brother-in-law, but that was the kind of news to tell her face to face, when they got back to London.

Anxiety rose up. Just how was she going to convince Santos that heading back to reality was *not* what he wanted to do?

CHAPTER EIGHT

THE SUN WAS hot by the time Georgina came up on deck, to find Santos relaxing, an empty coffee cup on the table. She hadn't yet seen him look quite this relaxed before, so at ease with life.

As if aware of her presence he turned to face her, and she wanted to hug her arms about her body, to shield herself from his appraising gaze. Instead she fought the urge, and when the wind blew the sheer kaftan against her like a second skin, revealing the tiny blue bikini she'd reluctantly put on, she walked towards him. As confident as any of the top models he'd dated, she smiled.

'It's so wonderful out here, away from everybody. I'd love to stay a bit longer.' She slid seductively into the seat opposite him, nerves tingling all over her body.

Anxiety, she told herself, refusing to acknowledge the fact that it was Santos who did that to her.

He looked past her briefly and she wondered if she'd gone too far. But a moment later a tray of breakfast and fresh coffee arrived. The crew were obviously back on board. Once they were alone again he turned his attention to her, his dark eyes sparkling like the sea in the morning sun.

'There would be one condition.' He poured coffee, the aroma reminding her of how little she'd eaten last night.

'And that would be…?' Her voice was flirty—the exact opposite of how she felt.

'The same as last night.'

'Last night…' she breathed, in a husky echo of his words as her body responded to the memory of his touch, his kisses.

He smiled, a dangerously seductive smile, and she all but melted. 'No pretence.'

'None at all?' She teased him with a coy smile, her fingers twining in her hair.

'I like the real Georgie.' He leant forward in his seat, his brows lifting suggestively. 'The Georgina you don't let the world see.'

She laughed a nervous laugh that made him smile even more, which in turn sent her heart thumping erratically. 'You make me sound fake—as if I'm a total fraud.'

'Not fake,' he said, and passed her a coffee.

She sipped it, thankful for something to do other than look into his handsome face.

'Just scared to let anyone know the real you.'

His words hit her with the precision of a marksman. Not letting the world see the real Georgina was just what she'd tried to do for the last five years. For so long that sometimes she forgot who she really was—forgot the woman with dreams of happiness. No, going there wasn't an option.

'Well, I guess we'll just have to spend time together— get to know one another a bit better.' She sipped her coffee and looked out at the sea, its ever-moving waves sparkling like diamonds, before turning her attention back to him.

'*Exactamente.*'

His gaze held hers, dark and passionate, sending shivers down her spine, and she wondered if she could do this. But if Emma was to stand any chance of making her wedding arrangements in peace she had to ensure they stayed in Spain.

'Thank you,' she said, alarmed at how husky her voice had suddenly become, how easily she could slip into the role of seductress.

'We'll sail further along the coast. There is a secluded cove we can stop at—a good place to swim in the sea.'

He smiled at her again. Her heart flipped over and butterflies took flight in her stomach. Perhaps it wouldn't be hard, keeping him occupied, because she really did want to. He was so very different from the man she'd first met in his office, the man her sister had talked of. This man consumed her very soul—made her want him and the dreams she'd long since forgotten.

'I'd like that.' A blush crept over her cheeks as she met his gaze before it slid down over her body, taking in all that the bikini did very little to hide.

'For my beautiful bride—anything.' He stood and leant down over her, his lips hovering tantalisingly close to hers as she looked up at him.

His breath was warm on her face and she resisted the need to close her eyes, wanting to see his. With excruciating slowness he brought his lips down onto hers, the sensation sending sparks of awareness all over her until she could only close her eyes, give in to the pleasure of his lips as they brushed gently over hers.

The kiss ended and he stood upright, dominating the sheltered outside area of the yacht. 'I will go and make arrangements while you enjoy breakfast.'

She watched him stride away, his casual jeans hugging his long legs to perfection. She shook her head briefly, trying to stop the images of last night, memories of his tanned body against her pale skin.

In a bid to quell her rising desire she turned her attention to the breakfast, not sure if she could eat anything. But the array of fresh fruit and the lure of warm croissants soon won her appetite over.

She became aware of the coastline receding, the yacht moving smoothly through gently rolling waves. Excitement fizzed inside her. It was like being young again.

She'd been happy before life had plunged her into a situation she really hadn't wanted. Her whole outlook on life had been carefree and full of adventure until the night her father had left. Now those memories were the reason she'd promised herself she'd never have children—because what would happen if she became like her mother? What would happen if she too went from one man to the next, looking endlessly for something that didn't exist, ignoring her children to the point of neglect?

'Why so sad, *querida*?'

Santos's accented voice shattered her thoughts as surely as if she'd been viewing them through a mirror.

'I was just remembering.' Quickly she tried to hide her emotions, recreate the impenetrable wall she hid behind, because right now her defences were low. Too low. And Santos was watching her with such unexpected sympathy she almost couldn't look at him.

'We all have things we shouldn't remember, but sometimes it helps to talk.'

His tone was soothing and reassuring. He sat next to her, taking her hand, his thumb stroking over the back of it gently. His concern as genuine as a lover's. She wanted to pull away, to distance herself from him. She felt utterly exposed, as if every emotion was completely visible to him.

'It was just my excitement as I realised the yacht was

moving,' she said, aware of the hoarseness in her voice. 'It's like being young again.'

He nodded once, his eyes full of understanding. 'What happened?'

'My mother found solace in the bottle after my father left.' Her heart thumped hard as pent-up anger flowed through her like a tidal wave—one that couldn't be halted now as it roared towards the shore. 'I had no choice but to care for Emma, try and shield her from it all. I had to grow up very quickly.'

'Shield her from what, Georgie?'

She looked up at him. His voice was now hard and controlled, his eyes narrowed and his brows pulling together in concentration.

She shouldn't be telling him this. It had nothing to do with him, and would serve no purpose whatsoever, but it was liberating to finally share it with someone.

'What was it, Georgina?' he urged as her silence lengthened.

He reached out and pushed back the hair from her face and she dropped her gaze, not wanting to see the sympathy in his eyes. How could a man as ruthless and in control as Santos possibly understand?

'Tell me, Georgie.'

One hand stroked her hair whilst the other held firmly onto her hand. She had no means of escape, no way out.

What would he think of her if she told him?

'At first she was just incapable of looking after us— that was unless she was in the throes of a new affair— but soon it was down to me to get Emma to school, to put a meal on the table.'

He stopped stroking her hair, his hand resting on her shoulder, warm and comforting. 'Go on.'

Those first words had unleashed all her hurt and she

knew she should stop. She shrugged, not wanting to allow him any closer emotionally.

'So I got out as soon as an opportunity presented itself. I had to. It was the only way of keeping a roof over our heads and food on the table. Any money my mother had was spent on what she considered important—not on what actually *was*, like food and rent.'

He sat back from her, his hands falling to his thighs, silent for a moment as he took in what she'd said. 'That opportunity being your marriage to Richard Henshaw?' His voice was hard, a slight growl in his throat.

She looked up at him. He really did think she'd married purely for the money and status Richard had given her. Words of defence were on the tip of her tongue, but something stopped her, froze them as if the warm sea breeze had changed to a bitter winter wind. Instead she wanted to tell him—wanted him to know.

'He offered me everything I wanted—and more.'

She sat taller in her seat and looked him in the eye. For a moment she'd almost told him the truth—told him how Richard had literally rescued her, offering her security for Emma and asking for nothing other than that she took his name. But sense had prevailed. If he wanted to think of her as a gold-digging socialite then he could.

'And, yes,' she added, with the haughty tone she knew made her sound so like the woman he thought she was re-sounding in her voice, 'I married him for his money and his status. But you can't accuse me of hiding that from you. Not when it is common knowledge.'

Santos's stomach hardened as his breath came fast. He clenched his teeth against an attack of jealousy as he imagined Georgina with another man—one she'd just admitted she'd had no feelings for. She hadn't attempted to hide the fact that she'd used a man who must have known he was ill when he married her.

She'd used Richard and she sat there now with the innocence of a child and waited for his reaction. He was angry with himself—angry at the irrational jealousy that raged inside him just thinking of her with another man. She was his wife, and what he felt for her now surpassed anything he'd felt for previous lovers.

'We all have a past, *querida*.' He kept his tone as nonchalant as possible, regretting having started the conversation. He'd known of her reputation when he'd agreed to their ludicrous deal, so why did it matter so much?

Control, he reminded himself. Whatever happened he had to be in control, and for a moment there he'd almost lost it—almost given in to the temptations of the devil. This whole episode was about getting what he wanted, not about emotions. Never emotions.

He stood up and walked to the side of the yacht, checking their location, almost relieved to see they had arrived at his chosen bay. He breathed deeply, enjoying the salty tang in his mouth, trying to revitalise himself before he turned back to look at the woman who was now his wife.

'Yes, we do. Including you.'

The accusation in her voice was clear and he couldn't help but smile at her pretence at fury. Her expression was severe, but her eyes were telling a different story.

'It's called life, Georgie.' He put out a hand and stepped towards her. 'And right now ours is for living. What about a swim in the sea? Wash all your troubles away?'

For a moment he thought she was going to refuse. Confusion furrowed her brow, then she regained her composure, took his hand and smiled up at him, openly flirting.

'A swim sounds delicious.'

Delicious. She was delicious, with the wind wrapping the almost see-through kaftan close to her glorious body, the blue bikini showcasing just what a figure she had. Lust thudded in his veins and he cursed his wayward thoughts.

'Something wrong?' A hint of a playful smile tugged her full lips up at the corners.

She knew exactly what was wrong, damn her.

'No. Unless it's wrong for a man to want to drag his wife back to bed instead of going swimming?' His voice was deep and guttural with the effort of reining in his libido.

She blushed and, as he had many times in the last few days, he wondered how she managed that little trick— how she managed to appear so innocent. 'I think we should swim first. It's not even midday yet.'

First.

She wanted him as much as he wanted her. Her darkening eyes were smouldering, giving him the message, setting fire to the embers of desire that had scorched his body last night. Never before had a woman affected him so much, made him want her so badly—but then never before had he had to wait so long to get a woman into his bed. And he certainly hadn't had to marry her to do so.

The irony of it wasn't lost on him as he felt her hand in his. It felt surprisingly good, as if it was right. 'I'll hold you to that,' he managed, despite the heat that raged within him. A swim in cold water was exactly what he needed.

He led her to the platform that had been lowered once the yacht was anchored and slipped off his deck shoes. Her gaze heated his blood as he pulled off his shirt, the sun instantly warm on his skin.

'Not joining me?' he teased, tugging off his jeans, amused by the blush that crept over her cheeks as her gaze slid down his body, resting on the evidence of just how aroused he had become at her loaded promise of what was to follow their swim.

The air crackled around them, their attraction as over-powering as if he hadn't touched her, hadn't tasted her skin or made her his. It was like the first time all over again, with anticipation raging in him like a bull.

He dived into the blue waters, and the rush of cold over his body was just what he needed. As he broke the surface he wiped water from his face and looked back up at Georgina, now sitting on the edge, feet dangling in the water, wearing only that very sexy blue bikini.

'It's cold!'

She laughed, her face lighting up, giving her an air of playful innocence, tugging at something deep within him.

'Only at first. Come on—you'll never know how good it is until you try it.' He trod water as he spoke, energised by the exercise and cold water.

Georgina watched, mesmerised, as his strong arms kept him exactly where he wanted to be. His strength and power were undeniable. She was behaving like a lovestruck teenager. Her heart was still pounding after that moment when he'd stood before her in his trunks, his tanned skin gleaming in the sun, the hardness of his arousal obvious. She wanted him with a ferocious need so alien that her breath had caught in her throat, and she'd been relieved when he'd expertly dived into the clear water. Relieved he had taken the temptation from her.

Cautiously she slipped into the water, gasping and laughing at the same time. 'It's so cold!' She tried hard to be sophisticated and serene, but all she managed was a fumbling splash.

'Only for a while,' Santos said, and in one stroke he moved towards her, encircling her body with his arm, keeping her safe and close. 'Like *you* were the day you propositioned me in my office.'

Shocked that he'd brought that up, she stopped moving her arms and immediately sank below the surface. His arm around her body pulled her back up, spluttering like a child.

'How dare you?' She tried to move away from him, back to the platform.

'Oh, I dare, *querida*—because it's true. You want everyone to think you are carved from ice, but you're not, are you?

She clutched the platform, gained a foothold on the ladder and pulled herself out of the water, then turned to face him as he looked up at her from the blue waves. 'Neither are you.'

'Can you blame me when you stand there like a sea goddess, water dripping from you in a most inviting way?'

'You're impossible.' The words rushed out, her frustration making her want to march away, but she couldn't tear her gaze from Santos as in one swift movement that made the muscles in his arms flex he hauled himself out of the sea.

Water ran down his tanned chest, trickling among his dark hair, heading downwards. She knew she shouldn't be looking, but she couldn't help herself. His thighs were strong and more dark hair lay flat against his wet skin, creating patterns all the way to his ankles. He was magnificent as he stood, sunlight gleaming on his skin.

He grabbed her hand and without a word headed back inside the yacht, leaving her little option but to follow. She couldn't say anything. The same sexual tension that had last night completely robbed her of the ability to think, let alone speak, raged around them.

In seconds they were alone in their suite, and only then did he let go of her hand. For a moment they looked at one another, gazes locked in some sort of primal dance. His chest rose and fell with the effort of breathing, just as hers did, and she knew instantly where this was going to end—and, worse, where she wanted it to end. He was an addiction.

With a muttered Spanish curse he turned and opened the door to the bathroom, and she watched through the doorway as he turned on the shower. She swallowed hard as he turned back to her, his expression almost fierce with control.

'Santos…' She managed a croaky whisper as he held out his hand to her. She took it and he pulled her hard against his wet body. Only then did she realise she was trembling.

'You're cold,' he said quietly, but she didn't miss the intensity in his voice.

She wasn't cold—not enough to tremble like this. It was him, and the electrified air that seemed to surround them.

'Come on.' He led her into the steam-filled bathroom and into the shower—one that had definitely been designed for two.

His hands slowly untied the bikini where it fastened at her neck, and each time his fingers touched her she had to suppress a shiver of pleasure. He let the thin straps go and peeled the wet material slowly away from her breasts, his gaze lingering enticingly on them.

He made a signal with his hands for her to turn around and slowly she did so, meeting the jets of warm water. Behind her she felt his hands as he released the final clasp of the bikini top and it dropped to the shower floor. Seconds later it was joined by his black trunks and her knees nearly buckled beneath her. Desire flooded her as he pressed his naked body against her back.

Instinctively her chin tilted up and she leant her head back against his shoulder, turning her face towards his. Hot, urgent lips claimed hers with such force she staggered forward, taking them both under the hot jets of water. His hands cupped her breasts and fire engulfed her, making her cry out with pleasure.

'You are the most desirable woman ever, *mi esposa.*'

He kissed down her neck, uttering words she didn't understand. But she did understand the desire and passion entwined with each one. A desire and passion that raged as wildly inside her.

'Santos, I want you.' Her voice was husky as his hands slid down her stomach, his fingers tugging at the ties on the side of the bikini briefs. As the material fell away his fingers moved towards the heated centre of her need for him and she arched away from him, trying to fight the ripple of pleasure from his touch.

With a suddenness that knocked all the breath from her body he turned her around, grasped her thighs, lifting her against him.

'Santos, it's never been like this before,' she gasped between ragged breaths as he lowered her onto him, plunging deeply and urgently inside her. She didn't care that she was telling him too much, giving away just how inexperienced she really was and how she was falling in love with him.

'Never?' The question rasped from him, halting her thoughts, as his fingers dug into her thighs, holding her where he wanted her.

She moved with him, encouraging him in this hot,

hard and primal dance. 'Never,' she gasped out as stars shattered around her so that instead of water coursing all over her it was stardust. 'Never. *Never.*'

As he found his release she clung to his body, trembling more now than she had when she'd stood before him in the bedroom just moments ago. He was breathing hard, his chest heaving against her tender breasts, one arm braced against the shower wall.

'At least we agree on something.' His voice, heavily accented, was a ragged whisper.

He released his vice-like grip on her thighs and she slid down, her legs so weak she wondered if she'd be able to stand. She couldn't. Her knees crumpled, but his arms were about her and in seconds he'd swept her up off her feet and left the shower.

Pausing briefly to grab a towel, he made his way to the bed. As if she were the most precious thing in the world he let her down to stand in front of him and then wrapped the white towel around her, heedless of his own wet body. Then he bent and kissed her lips so tenderly she thought she might actually cry. This was exactly what she'd abandoned all hope of ever finding, this warm, loving feeling.

Except this wasn't for real. This was just part of a deal, satisfying the attraction that had been arcing between them since that very first meeting. It was also the only way she knew of keeping Santos from heading back to the villa and maybe London.

'You're still wet,' she whispered, not wanting to analyse her motives or question her dreams now.

He stepped back from her and started rubbing his hands over the towel to dry her. This was getting too intense, too close to being like a proper romance, so great was the attraction she felt for him. Her breath shuddered as he pulled the towel from her and dried himself off.

And all the while his gaze held hers, the passion and desire still flowing between them evident in the depths of his eyes.

He picked her dressing gown off the bed, now remade after their night of passion, and handed it to her. 'You must care for your sister very much.'

Instantly her senses were on high alert. What was he suggesting? 'She's all I have.'

He handed her the cream silk garment. 'But to marry just so that your sister can marry for love?' His voice rose with incredulity as he took fresh clothes from the wardrobe and hastily got dressed.

'Maybe I love my sister as much as you hate your brother.' Was he referring to their marriage or her first one? It made no difference; both had been made out of love for her sister.

Tension filled the room and his eyes sparked with anger as he stood in front of her, all the passion and desire of moments ago forgotten.

'Half-brother.' The words were harsh and staccato.

She pulled on the dressing gown, no longer wanting him to see her naked now he was clothed, as if it somehow weakened her. He turned and paced across the room towards the door, but she couldn't let him go, couldn't let him walk out now, even if it meant killing the loving moments they'd shared.

'Coward.' The word rushed from her lips, provoking him.

Instantly he whirled round and fixed her with a fierce glare, his face a hardened and angry mask. 'I don't do emotions, Georgina. Hate or love. I don't do them.'

'And because of that two people who love one another are suffering.'

'How?' He strode back across the room, but she stood

her ground. 'And how do you know they are in love? How do they even know?'

'You must have loved someone, Santos, despite what you just said.'

'Love is for weak-willed fools.' His voice was like granite and his eyes glittered dangerously as he looked at her.

'You don't really believe that?' she whispered in disbelief.

She'd vowed she'd never love anyone other than Emma, never give her heart to a man as her mother had time and time again. But somehow she'd become dangerously close to loving Santos.

'Isn't that why you made this damn deal, Georgina, because you don't believe in love?' He was like an angry lion, caged up and looking for a way out as he strode across the room to glance out of the window. He turned and looked at her, waiting for her reply.

'I did it *for* love.' She rallied against his contempt. 'I did it for the love of my sister.'

'Ha!' He laughed, so arrogantly she almost cringed. 'You did it for money, for all you could get from it—just as you did the first time around.'

How dared he bring Richard into this? The man who had seen she needed a lifeline and offered one without expecting anything in return? Well, if that was what he thought of her, so be it. Attack was the best form of defence.

'Yes, just as I did the first time.'

For a moment he looked at her in stunned silence, his jaw grinding hard. He looked for all the world as if he was jealous of Richard. How could a powerful man like Santos be jealous of anything or anyone?

He glared at her. 'Get dressed,' he snapped after what seemed like an eternity. 'We're going back to the villa.'

Panic tore at her. She'd promised Emma she'd keep him out of the way, and here on the yacht was the perfect place.

'So soon?' She hated the nervous edge to her voice, but knew any attempts at flattering him would be futile.

His eyes narrowed. 'I have work to do. Playing at this newlywed game has gone on for long enough.'

With that he strode from the room and she sank onto the bed. Last night they had made love for the first time, been given pleasure so intense it still lingered in her body. Only minutes ago they had been consumed by desire and need for one another. How could the man who kissed her so passionately be the same man who'd just left the room?

She dragged in a deep breath, pressing her fingertips to her lips, bruised from his hard kisses in the shower. How could she, a woman who'd renounced love, feel such desolation as the man she'd given herself to last night with total completeness walked out on her?

CHAPTER NINE

SANTOS'S MOOD WAS as dark as the storm clouds rolling down from the mountains. He'd thought Georgina was different, thought she could keep emotions out of things. Instead she'd proved beyond doubt that she was as clingy as any woman, unable to resist the urge to delve into his past.

He'd thought he'd met his match—a woman who could share his passion without the need for anything more.

But he'd been wrong, damn it, very wrong.

'I have business matters to attend to.'

Unable to keep the frustration from reverberating in his voice as they arrived back at the villa, he swung the car in through the gates without giving the photographers loitering there a second glance and powered up the driveway.

Georgina was silent next to him, but he could feel her watching him. He couldn't look at her now. She'd already proved just what an effect she had on him, proved how easily she could distract him.

'I'll get ready to go back to London.' Her voice was quiet, but firm.

'London?' The car halted abruptly as he fought for control. His fingers curled hard around the leather of the steering wheel as he gripped it even harder. One thing was for certain: she was not going back to London. Not yet.

'It's what I'd planned once the world knew we were married.' Her voice still had a husky edge to it, but strength and determination echoed there too.

That unsettled him even more. She seemed able to shut off and return to icy control much more easily than he was able to do. The carefree hours they'd spent on the yacht meant his usual detached approach to relationships was eluding him. And he didn't like it.

Santos looked at her lips, full and still very kissable. Fire leapt to life deep within him—a ferocious burning need to take her straight to his bed once more. It was more than lust, this need to be with her. He gritted his teeth; he had to be as collected as she was right now.

'That is what you *originally* planned, Georgina.' He tossed the words carelessly at her, trying to appear as unaffected by her as possible as he turned off the engine and got out of the car. 'But it is not what we finally agreed on.'

She got out of the car, all elegance and poise, then faced him across the shiny red roof. She looked stunning, sexy, and very different from the woman he'd brought here just a few days ago. Her eyes were bright, her skin lightly tanned and her hair looked tousled, as if she'd just got out of his bed.

'I'm going home, Santos.' Her words were clipped as she slammed the car door shut.

'You *are* home. You agreed to live as my wife, to be by my side, and right now I'm here.'

Not wanting to discuss it further, he locked the car and marched into the house, heading straight for his study. The sound of her footsteps on the marble floor would have told him she was following even if his body hadn't tingled so wildly, alerting him to her presence.

'Look, Santos…' She practically purred as she followed him into the sanctuary of his study. Hell, she was good at this—good at putting on a show of whatever she wanted people to see. Anger, gentleness or hot desire, it didn't matter—she was an accomplished actress through and through. 'Is there really a need to keep up this pretence?'

He thought of the clause of his father's will, the way it had pushed him into not only marrying but considering having a child, an heir. Frustration mixed with his anger and he pushed the thought roughly aside.

'It was in the agreement.' He kept his words firm as he headed to the filing cabinet and the file containing copies of their pre-nuptial agreement.

'I did not sign anything to say I would stay by your side like a faithful puppy dog. You must be mistaken, Santos.' Her eyes sparked fury at him, their colour lightening to a brilliant bronze, and her voice had a sharp edge to it, but she still looked sexy, still made his body ache for her.

If she continued to stand there like that, her hand on her hip, her lips almost pouting, he'd have to kiss her. And if he did that he'd never stop. She was like an addiction.

He turned his back on her, opened the cabinet drawer and pulled out the folder, tossing it on the desk so that the contents slipped from it, spreading across the table like a pack of cards. 'Take a look.'

Her gaze dropped from his face to the documents, then back to his. 'I know what I signed.' Her voice wavered slightly. 'But we've done what we set out to do. If I have to stay here then at least let me ring Emma, tell her she and Carlo can set a date.'

He inhaled deeply. He had to tell her just what else he needed from the marriage.

Her phone rang and she delved into her bag and pulled it out. For a moment she looked at it, then at him. 'It's Emma,' she said as the ringing ceased. 'What do I tell her? That we are happily married so they can be the same?'

He cursed harshly and paced to his window, taking in the view of the mountains almost obscured by dark clouds laden with the promise of a storm. The air was heavy and he knew that at any moment it would break.

He cursed again and dragged his fingers through his hair with an unaccustomed feeling of tumultuous emotions. What the hell had happened to him to make him feel so out of control?

He'd got married. One of the two things in the world he'd never wanted to do. The second was to become a father, and now it seemed his hand was to be forced there too unless he could find another way.

Again he raked his hands through his hair. He couldn't think straight. The air was becoming heavier and more oppressive by the minute and he could feel Georgina's gaze fully on him, expectantly waiting for an answer.

'Tell her to arrange their wedding.' His words were sharp, and it was an effort to keep his frustration at the situation he now found himself in from showing. Damn it, he still couldn't tell her why she had to stay.

Her gaze locked with his, the soft brown eyes that had almost melted his soul as he'd made her his now burnished like copper, angry and glittering. He clenched his hands and met her challenging gaze.

'This is what you wanted all along, isn't it?' What was she waiting for now? His blessing for the marriage?

'You know it is…'

A *but* seemed to linger in the air with as much threat as the storm he could feel waiting to erupt.

He raised a brow at her, finally slipping back into his professional mode. 'Anything else?'

She shook her head, a look of disappointment crossing her face and he bit down hard on the sudden urge to go to her, to hold her and make everything right. Because he couldn't. He would never be able to make this right—for Georgina or himself.

She stood tall and resolute for a few more seconds, her gaze fixed to his, then she left, taking with her some of the pressure that dominated the room.

He needed to contact his legal team. There just had to be a way out of that final clause. Satisfied he'd sorted the situation for now, he turned on his laptop. He had far too many emails to answer, but the first one snared his attention with such ferocity he dropped down into his chair.

It was offering him congratulations on his marriage. Just what they had planned. But it was the last line that almost made his heart stop. He and Georgina weren't the only couple to have got married.

Blood pounded in his ears, the sound so loud it almost masked the first rumble of thunder as the storm finally broke.

It couldn't be true.

Quickly he scanned the headlines and within minutes found confirmation that, yes, it was true. He'd been tricked, manipulated, and totally played for a fool. He wanted to rage and shout, but one thing life had taught him was that rushing in without first knowing all the facts could leave him in a weak position.

No, this had to be approached with caution. He had to know what part Georgina had played in this. Instinct told him it was a very big part. He was angry he'd lowered his defences enough for her to see the man he really was. For the first time ever he'd felt the stirrings of something he'd shut out of his life long ago and had almost been fooled into opening that door.

Georgina slipped outside to the pool. The clouds were dark and heavy. It looked as if a storm was brewing, and she hated storms—she'd never shaken off her childhood fear of them. Despite the dark clouds that hung low in the sky she settled on a lounger by the pool, her need to speak with Emma greater than her desire to hide from the storm. She could hardly wait to hear her sister's squeal of delight when she told her they could set a date.

'Georgie.' Emma sounded different somehow as she answered the phone. 'Where are you?'

'I'm still in Spain, and you can get set a date for your wedding.' She took a breath, putting on an air of jubilation—one she was far from feeling. 'Santos and I—we're married.'

Emma hesitated, and a shiver of apprehension slipped down Georgina's spine as the silence lengthened down the phone connection.

Finally Emma spoke, sounding oddly far away. 'I know. It's all over town.'

At least her plan had worked, Georgina consoled herself. All she could hope for now was that Emma would believe that she and Santos had married because of the attraction they had for one another, after the whirlwind romance that had started at the party.

'Georgie...'

Emma's voice sounded nervous, and as the silence lengthened still further Georgina heard the first rumble of thunder. 'Georgie, Carlo and I...we got married a few days ago.'

Georgina almost dropped the phone with shock. Her

quiet, biddable sister had gone against everyone and married in secret, without even telling *her*. Hurt lanced through her as she thought of the day she'd always imagined for Emma—a day when she would be there to see her married, not on a yacht off the coast of Spain.

A flash of lightning made Georgina's heart-rate accelerate wildly, but she tried to keep it under control. She didn't want Emma to worry—didn't want her to know of the ramifications her actions.

'Georgie, are you still there?'

She could hear the unease in her sister's voice and tried to focus her mind. How could Emma have betrayed her?

'I have to go, Emma, there's a storm coming. I'll call you later.'

She cut the connection as the full implications of what this meant hit home.

And Santos. What would *he* think?

A low rumble of thunder followed by the first heavy drops of rain made her retreat to the safety of the villa. Her fear of the storm outweighed the fact that Santos was himself like a brewing storm—one she didn't want to be around when it broke. From the doorway she watched the raindrops falling into the pool, disturbing its smooth surface. Deep down she knew she had more than a storm to fear.

The temperature dropped and a cool wind picked up. The white curtains billowed into the room where she stood, watching the increasingly heavy rain. Lightning lit up the darkening sky and she shuddered in a breath, as tense as the air around her. The clap of thunder was so loud she had to suppress a scream as she beat a hasty retreat further into the villa, feeling as shaken by Emma's revelation as by the storm itself. The trembling of her hands was very real.

'Scared of the storm?' Santos's voice was clipped and hard. 'Or is this another of your wonderful acting roles?'

She frowned, blinking in confusion as he came to stand before her. His dark eyes were full of fury and as he folded his arms across his chest and looked down at her she saw visible tension in his neck and shoulders.

'A little,' she lied, and rubbed her hands up and down her arms as if she were cold, refusing to rise to the bait of his last comment.

His gaze darted to the movement, watching through narrowed eyes, then moved back to her face. She fought the way her body responded to him, despite her apprehension about telling him what she'd just found out. She took a deep breath and tried to focus herself, curb her fear of the storm and deny the need to be held by him, to feel safe in his arms.

He marched past her and closed the doors to the terrace. The curtains ceased their wild dance but the tension of the storm remained, wrapping itself around them, drawing them towards each other. His dark gaze met hers and defiantly she lifted her chin, straightened her back, determined not to show him her fear.

There were two storms raging, she realised with a sinking feeling. Two storms she was going to have to ride out, no matter what. There wasn't any escape from either now.

'Your plan worked,' he said as he stood with his back to the doors and the lashing rain.

The dark clouds behind him only intensified the image of anger he projected.

'My plan was for Emma to think we were lovers so she wouldn't question our marriage.' Her voice didn't sound as firm as she wanted, and anxiety made her stomach flutter. She had to regain her composure.

'And why was that so important, Georgina?'

The use of her full name hurt, somehow, and the light sarcasm in his voice was unmistakable.

'You openly admit to marrying for financial security once already—why would she question *our* marriage?'

She watched his jaw tighten as he took in a deep breath, as if he was holding back what he really wanted to say. 'She never knew I married Richard so that I could fund her education and give her a secure home. My first marriage isn't part of this, Santos.'

Thunder cracked overhead, the villa seeming to shake with the force of it. Georgina glanced anxiously around the room, thankful that she was no longer out at sea.

'It damn well is when your reputation precedes you.' His voice was hard and echoed the aggression of the storm. The expression on his face was as dark and brooding as the sky.

'My reputation?' Lightning lit the room and her heart thudded almost as loudly as the thunder. 'If by that you mean that I married Richard, an older and unwell man, because he offered me lifelong security in return for a few years of companionship, then, yes, my reputation does precede me.'

She glared at him, hardly able to believe they were discussing her first marriage when it was the marriage of his brother to her sister that should take precedence. That was the one that affected them both, whether they liked it or not.

She had to tell him, but anxiously kept the conversation on its current course. As the next crack of thunder threatened to shake the foundations of the villa she stood her ground, glaring at Santos.

'A companionship so loving that you were dating other

men just weeks after his funeral.' He practically snarled the words at her, so intense was his anger.

'It was what he wanted,' she said, softly but firmly, remembering how insistent Richard had been that she should move on in life, find herself a man she could love.

She'd dated a few men just to do as Richard had wanted, to honour the memory of the man who'd given her a future. But she hadn't enjoyed their company and very quickly gossip had started.

After the initial shock of being at the centre of everyone's speculation she'd soon realised it provided a wall to hide behind.

'I found out very quickly that seeing a man once or twice only was the best way.' Let him think the worst of her. She had other worries right now. Besides, if he believed that of her it would keep him at arm's length—something she had to do now no matter what. She couldn't dwell on the closeness they'd shared.

Santos's brow furrowed. 'Best way for what?' The words snapped from him.

'For doing what *you* do,' she flung at him as another rumble of thunder, just as intense, reverberated around the room. 'For keeping the world at bay, keeping the gossips with something to get their teeth into, because ultimately it meant I could be on my own. I never wanted to be married the first time and I certainly don't want to be married now.'

She flopped down onto the sofa, unable to fight any longer. Remaining indifferent to what was being said about her and the shock of what Emma had done was finally too much.

How could her sister have said nothing? How could she have sneaked away the moment she'd left for Spain? It was a complete and utter betrayal. Emma had as good as thrown everything she'd ever done for her back in her face.

Santos walked across the marble floor. A hint of softness entered his tone as he crouched before her, forcing her to look into his eyes. 'Then why offer yourself to me?'

She swallowed down the urge to cry, to collapse into an emotional heap, and looked into his eyes. Their dark depths were almost unreadable. He was so close, and the spark of attraction passing between them was as strong as ever, but she mustn't let that cloud her mind and muddle her judgement.

'Why, Georgina?' he prompted, his voice a little firmer, and she realised the anger she'd seen in him earlier was still simmering beneath the surface.

She took a breath to tell him what she'd just learnt, but couldn't. The look in his glittering eyes halted those words

'For Emma,' she began, trying to put off the moment just a little longer. 'She believes in the dream of love, the happy-ever-after, and it's Carlo—your brother—who is that dream for her. When she told me about the will it seemed the most obvious deal to make. I'd married for convenience for Emma's benefit once before. I could do it again.'

Georgina was emotionally wrung out, but she had to tell him. She didn't want to—didn't want to rouse his anger—but she knew she had to. She couldn't keep it from him. He had a right to know.

'They are already married.'

The words were out before he had a chance to say anything.

He studied her for a moment, crouching in front of her as if he was talking to a child, making her think he'd be good with children. An image of her holding a baby with Santos's dark eyes and complexion rushed into her mind, not for the first time in recent days, but she pushed it harshly away. Marrying him was one thing, but she'd never have his child. She could never have a child, full-stop. She didn't want to risk being as useless as her own mother.

'When did you know?' His words, although cajoling, still reverberated with anger.

She looked down at the phone she still clutched in her hand and sighed. 'Minutes ago.'

Betrayal ripped through her again at the thought of what Emma and Carlo had done, but she knew Emma would never have done it alone—never.

'I can't believe it,' she whispered, more to herself than Santos.

'They married on Saturday.'

He stood up and looked down on her, his height making her feel small, his words like hailstones raining down on her. Another rumble of thunder followed, echoing his anger.

'Saturday?' She blinked back tears as she thought of Emma getting married whilst she'd been flying out to Spain. Then it hit her. 'That means Carlo married first.'

He nodded, folding his arms across his chest once more.

'So our marriage was for nothing. Carlo inherits the business and I miss the biggest day of my sister's life.' She wanted to jump up, to stand and face him, but her knees were too weak so she just buried her face in her hands.

What was she going to do now? Santos probably thought she'd conspired with them to outsmart him. There was only one thing she could do. Go home. Get far away from Santos.

'I'll go and pack,' she said, finally finding the strength to stand as another rumble filled the room, this time sounding as if it was finally receding.

'No.'

Santos grabbed her arm as she made to leave and she looked up into his face. A small part of her wanted to see the gentleness she'd seen on their wedding night. She wanted to feel as special as he'd made her feel that night. But instead his eyes were brittle with hardness.

'You are my wife. You will stay here.'

She shook her head. 'No, Santos, I can't. Their marriage changes everything.'

'Your scheming, meaning that Carlo married first, has changed nothing. We are still married.'

He held her arm tight, pulling her against his body. She could feel the heat of it and, despite the anger and tension in the air, her body responded traitorously to his.

'It's all about the business for you, isn't it?' Accusation rang in her voice as she lifted her chin, finding her defiant streak once more, denying the burning need that raged inside her. 'You can't bear it that you've lost it.'

He shook his head and his voice was hard. 'I haven't lost it. Not yet. And we will remain married.'

'Why?' Her breath was heaving in her chest.

His eyes darkened, the brittleness of earlier replaced with hot desire.

'Because of this.'

Before she could question him further his mouth claimed hers in a hot, searing kiss. She gasped in a mixture of annoyance and pleasure as his hand cupped her breast, making her arch against him, only being held upright by the firm grasp of his hand on her arm. She had no escape. Neither did she want an escape. She wanted his touch, his kiss. Damn it, she wanted *him*. She wanted him because she loved him—and that was exactly why she had to go.

She could hardly think straight, let alone put coherent words together, as he broke the kiss and looked down at her.

'This undeniable attraction that exists between us. We can't fight it for ever.'

'No,' she managed in a croaky voice. 'But it can't last for ever.'

He shrugged, relinquishing his grip on her arm to hold her hand instead. 'True, but we can explore it while it lasts.'

'Why would I want to do that?' Indignation at his knowing glance leapt through her.

'Because we are man and wife,' he said in a smooth tone that rippled over her heightened senses like velvet. 'Truly man and wife.'

She shook her head. 'Not really, we aren't. It was just a deal. Just a marriage of convenience.'

'Was our wedding night on the yacht just part of the deal?'

His self-satisfied smile made her blush at the memory of just how abandoned she'd been. He kissed her—a brief but intense one.

'I thought not.'

'No, Santos.' She pushed at his chest, needing space to think. 'This isn't what I wanted. Neither of us did. And now Emma and Carlo have married there is no need for us to be together.'

'That's where you are wrong, because Carlo hasn't yet inherited the business.'

'Of course he has. He's married—before you.' She almost froze with shock. Some of his earlier words were now making sense, like his accusation of her acting. He'd been playing with her.

'Yes, they are married.' The smile didn't reach his eyes this time. 'But, *querida*, that doesn't change anything.'

'What do you mean?' Confused, she stopped pushing him away. She didn't understand. Emma and Carlo had got married before she and Santos had even arrived in Spain, making Carlo the first son to marry. 'Why doesn't it change anything?'

Santos struggled with his conscience. Her act of being the wounded party was very convincing, just as her act of fear of the storm had been, but he didn't believe she'd known nothing of their plans. Why else would she have asked so seductively to stay on the yacht longer, or even agreed to leave London with him, if not to make it as difficult as possible for him to contact the outside world? She'd practically thrown herself at him, used all that a woman could to snare his interest and keep him from going back to the villa. She'd made him want her, teased and dallied with his desire since that first kiss at the party, and there was only one reason as far as he was concerned.

She'd planned it all along.

True, she'd wanted him as much as he'd wanted her. He'd have to be blind and stupid not to see how her body responded to his slightest touch. And each time he'd kissed her the attraction between them had intensified, until they couldn't ignore it any longer.

She'd deceived him, duped him, like all females did, with her body. And just like his father he'd ignored everything to be with her, to make her his. He'd been like a man possessed, unable to think of anything else other than Georgina. Thoughts of her had been all-consuming.

He enjoyed being with women, but never had he been so completely under a woman's spell.

Even now, when her kisses tasted of deceit, he wanted her. Passion burned in her eyes as she stood and glared at him. How dared she look so wounded? There could only be one winner in this game of passion and deceit she'd started. And that would be him.

'It isn't the first son to marry who inherits.' The words slipped out effortlessly. Finally he'd got her attention. 'But the first married son to produce an heir.'

He watched as his words slowly filtered through, like water permeating through limestone, until finally the expression on her face told him she understood the full implications.

She shook her head, backing away from him as if he was evil itself, her beautiful face ashen white, her eyes wide with disbelief. Oh, but she was a good actress. He almost believed it. Almost.

CHAPTER TEN

THE FIRST MARRIED son to produce an heir.

No, she screamed in her head, whilst outwardly the shutters came down, cocooning her behind a safe barrier.

'How long have you known this?' How could he stand there so calmly and tell her that? He might as well say her whole plan had been a waste of time. He'd lied all this time, but she couldn't see a trace of remorse.

'Long enough.'

His words sent a shiver down her spine.

'So what were you hoping for? A honeymoon baby?' She wanted to close her eyes against the pain of shattered dreams as they splintered around her. For just one night she'd thought she could sample that dream. She hadn't expected her attraction for him to turn into something deeper. Now it was spoilt by his admissions. His deceit. 'No wonder you were so—what was it?—unusually *relaxed* about contraception.'

'That's absurd.'

His eyes looked dark and hostile but she stood tall, remaining as defiant as she could manage.

A ray of sunlight speared the gloom and she glanced out at the clearing sky, glad that at least one storm was over.

'Not absurd, Santos.' She looked directly at him, something akin to anger and disappointment flitting through her. 'Not when you consider the clause of the will and that you knew Carlo wanted to get married. He loves my sister. Just by marrying he was a threat to you—because not only would he be the first married son, but probably the first married son to have the required heir.'

It was like a puzzle, and finally she was putting it together. She still had a few pieces to find, but it was all beginning to make sense now.

'Why are you so against Carlo?' She felt frustrated by those missing pieces. 'When you could have married any one of the women you've dated in the past and inherited everything you believe is yours.'

She watched as he paced the room—long, lean strides that drew her attention. As if needing escape, he opened the doors to the terrace and strode out. The fresh smell of dampness after the rain rushed into the room as he left. For a moment she stood and watched him, saw his pain, his frustration, with every move he made, and something deep inside her tugged at her emotions.

She knew that kind of pain, that kind of emptiness.

She walked to the door. Santos stood looking out to sea, his broad shoulders tense and the muscles in his arms taut as he leant on the balustrade. She longed to go to him, to touch him and soothe his pain. But sense prevailed. This was all of his making. She couldn't let him know how she felt—not when he'd used everyone as pawns in his power game.

It rushed at her so hard she almost stumbled. All her breath momentarily left her body and her heart raced like a wild horse fleeing captivity.

It couldn't be true—it just couldn't.

She loved him. Completely and utterly.

She pressed her fingertips to her lips to stifle a cry of distress. She didn't want to love anyone. She *couldn't* love anyone. And certainly not Santos Ramirez. Since the day her father had turned his back on them she'd watched her mother take a path of self-destruction. Her parents' actions proved beyond doubt that love was all-consuming, but also that it hurt, left you alone and killed all joy in life when it went wrong. It was a gamble she'd never wanted to take, so how had it happened? How had she fallen in love with Santos?

'I'm not against Carlo.'

His harsh words dragged her mind back from the pain of her past.

'Just the marriage.'

She sensed his vulnerability as he remained with his back to her, looking out to sea, at the sky clearing and brightening after the storm. Knowing she shouldn't, but unable to stop herself, she crossed the terrace and stood by him, her shoulder almost touching his arm as she stood surveying the view.

'Why did your father put such a clause in his will, forcing you to marry?' This was something that had niggled at her since Emma had first mentioned it. She'd imagined two young boys vying for their father's attention. A man who didn't deserve any from either of them as far as she was concerned.

'It's a family business, started by my grandfather—my mother's father. I suppose he assumed that as I was older by nine years I'd marry and have a family a long time before Carlo did.'

He sounded resigned and it tugged at her heart to hear him, almost as if he was admitting defeat.

'He must have thought he was being fair to us both, putting that clause in his will.'

'So why didn't you marry?' The question just had to

be asked. He'd never been short of female company. She'd very quickly learnt that.

He turned to face her and she held her breath as he looked down at her. His eyes searched her face as if looking for answers to questions he didn't even know. She watched as his face set into hard lines, shutting her out.

'To avoid the mess we are in now.' The angry words all but barked out at her.

She shivered despite the sun. 'It's easy to sort out.' Her words were curt as she lifted her chin in defiance and challenge, the softer emotions quashed by his frozen expression. 'I leave and you file for divorce.'

In one swift stride he came towards her, his hand holding her arm firmly. 'You are not going anywhere unless I do—and as for a divorce…'

He spoke with a voice so stern and disapproving she blinked in shock.

'There will not be a divorce. Your meddling has made sure of that.'

'But—' she began, wondering what she wanted to try and tell him, even what she didn't. 'There isn't any reason to remain married—not now.'

'You are forgetting, *mi esposa*, that an heir may yet still be needed.' He let go of her, keeping her where she stood with just the fixed glare of his dark eyes.

'No,' she snapped, and backed away from him, bumping against the chair she'd sat in to call her sister earlier. 'Even you're not so cold and callous that you'd bring a child into the world just to inherit a business.'

'I had hoped not even to marry to inherit. When you so kindly offered yourself I believed it would be enough, that I could find a way out of the clause long before Carlo married. But your meddling has changed everything.'

His eyes glittered furiously at her but she held her

ground, squared her shoulders and met his accusation head on.

Her *meddling*? 'What do you mean?'

'Don't play the innocent with me.'

His eyes glittered dangerously but she refused to be intimidated, refused to back down.

'Not when you've led me on, driven me wild with need for you since the night of the party.'

'I did not lead you on.' Indignation flared to life in her and she almost stamped her foot in frustration.

Santos knew he was losing his patience, reaching the boiling point that very few people managed to push him to. All he wanted was to prevent her from leaving. He needed her, yes, but he wanted her more.

'So what was our wedding night if not to divert my attention and keep me out of the way?'

She gasped at him, a blush creeping over her cheeks, and she looked as if she was struggling for words.

'You must have been delighted when I took you to the yacht. What better place to keep me out of the way?' Humiliation burned through him like a forest fire. He'd been used, played for a fool, and it wounded him even more to think that he'd relaxed. He'd wanted to open up to her, wanted to be who he really was, when all along she'd been as fake as snow in the desert. 'You flirted yourself at me in an attempt to stay longer on the yacht.'

Her brow furrowed and pain and confusion swirled in her eyes. For a moment he wanted to reach for her, wanted to kiss it all away. But kissing had got him into this mess. Kissing and much more had left him emotionally exposed and vulnerable.

'If that's what you think, Santos, it would be much better if you just let me go home. Alone.' Her words were firm and devoid of any emotion.

'That,' he snapped, instantly reining himself back, 'is not negotiable. You will stay here with me now I know where Carlo and Emma are.'

'Where they are?' She spoke rapidly, shock sounding in her tone. 'You mean they're not in London?'

Was it possible he'd got it all wrong? That she'd known nothing of their marriage plans?

He moved away from her—away from the intensity of her eyes and the questions deep within them. Maybe sending her back to London alone would be for the best, enable him to think clearly. Because his need for her had increased since they'd spent the night together and each time she came close his body remembered, even if his mind refused to acknowledge what he was beginning to feel for her.

'Perhaps you can tell me.' He tossed the words across the terrace as he made his way back inside the villa. 'You can explain everything to me on our way out this evening.'

'There's only one place I'm going this evening and that's the airport—with or without your help.' He knew she had followed him inside. He could feel her, sense her.

He sat down on the sofa, stretching his arm along the back of the black leather, and watched as she stood, fury blazing from her, in the centre of the room. A smile twitched the corners of his lips despite the bitter taste of humiliation. She looked stunningly sexy, a little fireball of passion.

'Tonight we are expected at a party my cousin has arranged for us and I have no intention of arriving without my bride.'

'Well, I'm sorry to disappoint you, Santos, but your bride is leaving. Right now.'

He clenched his jaw as his mind raced. 'You can't. You signed the agreement. You have legally agreed to live as my wife for twelve months.'

Her eyes widened in shock. 'I don't believe you actually put that in. You're barbaric.'

'I need an heir, Georgina.'

Right there in front of him she seemed to deflate. All the fire and fury drained from her and he sat forward, his elbows on his knees. Was she actually going to faint?

'I can't give you what you want.'

The anguish in her voice alarmed him and he leapt up and stood before her.

'I can't have a baby—I can't.'

Can't have a baby.

He hadn't considered this. He'd assumed that, like almost every woman, she'd want to become a mother.

'Why not?'

This threw everything into turmoil. If Carlo and Emma returned from Vegas as parents-to-be he would have lost everything—exactly what he'd promised his mother he'd never do the last time he saw her. Although he still didn't know what kind of misguided loyalty made him want to keep that promise.

Large tears welled up in Georgina's eyes. One broke free and ran down her cheek. Santos didn't know what to do. He hadn't considered the possibility that she couldn't have children. She'd been so adamant that she'd do anything to enable her sister to marry. He'd seen her as a viable back-up plan—a marriage of convenience to a woman who would be the mother of his child, should that drastic step be needed.

'I can't…I just can't,' she croaked in a whisper, tugging at something deep inside him so much that he wanted to hold her close, to soothe her.

Instead he clenched his hands into fists and marched away from her. 'This changes nothing. You are my wife. You agreed to it for one year and I'm not going to allow you to publicly humiliate me any further. I don't need my wife deserting me within days of our supposed whirlwind romance. It's bad enough that Carlo and Emma have run off to Vegas…'

'Vegas?' Incredulity made her tear-laden eyes widen and he steeled himself against the need to hold her.

'As if you didn't know.'

Attack was the only way he could control the myriad of strange new emotions running riot inside him. He wanted her with him, yet he didn't. Above all he wanted to punish her for her part in deceiving him, but even *he* wasn't so callous that in the face of what she'd just told him he'd actually do that.

Vegas. Emma had gone to Las Vegas to get married.

'I didn't know,' Georgina whispered, betrayal rushing through her.

They must have planned it for weeks. Why hadn't Emma said something? Taken her into her confidence?

He took her hand, his mood softened. 'It seems we are both victims of their deception.'

His deep voice sent shivers of awareness down her spine, but she remained firm and resolute, not trusting him.

'Have you spoken to Carlo?' She pulled back, watching his face as she asked the question.

'No, but the gossip columns are full of it. When we left for Spain they must have gone straight to Vegas. They must have left as soon as we'd left the party. Damn it, they knew all along.'

He let go of her as his frustration built again and she felt strangely alone. The touch of his hand had been grounding, somehow. He blamed her for what Emma and Carlo had done, that much was obvious, yet still she wanted his comfort, wanted to feel his arms around her.

If she was going to survive the next few days she had to push her emotions right to the back of her mind—had to ignore them before they exposed her to the biggest pain of all. One thing she was sure of: she couldn't remain his wife for a year—not if it meant living with him.

Twice in her life she had trusted and loved a man and twice he had let her down. Her father, whom she'd adored, had walked away one stormy night without a backward glance, leaving her in tears, clinging to the front door. Then Richard, whom she'd loved in a gentle, appreciative way, had left her alone in the world—more alone than she cared to admit.

Now Santos.

She'd fallen in love with him so passionately and deeply she couldn't even think properly any more. Her usual unemotional demeanour was smashed into icy crumbs.

'Emma would never have done it if she'd thought it would end like this.' She tried to think back to all they'd spoken off when they'd been getting ready for the party Santos had thrown. She shook her head in disbelief. 'She just wouldn't.'

'It would seem your sister isn't as loyal to you as you are to her.' Santos's voice was hard as he paced the room. 'Whatever possessed them to run off and get married?'

'Love,' Georgina whispered.

Santos rounded on her. 'Love is for fools. It destroys lives.'

'How can you say that?' Her frustration matched his fury and she glared at him, daring him to answer. 'You must have loved once.'

An echo of a previous conversation filled her mind.

He closed the distance between them in long strides, dominating the room with his volatile mood. 'Your father walked out on you, no?' His accent was stronger than ever as he battled with his emotions.

Her breath caught in her throat as he brought up her past, made the memories of that night—already too fresh after the storm—rush back. 'My father has nothing to do with it.'

'If he'd loved you he wouldn't have left. That's what you think, no?'

His eyes locked with hers, holding her prisoner, forcing her to face things she didn't want to face.

Before she could answer his harsh words came at her again, as if he no longer cared what he was saying. 'It's the same for me. Love will never be a part of how I think of my mother, or she of me.' He whirled around and marched back outside, as if needing more space to vent his anger.

Cautiously she followed him outside. 'What happened with your mother?' Her words were a whisper as she watched him drag in a deep breath.

He turned to look at her once more, his face set in firm lines.

'I was a mistake.' He swallowed as if the words tasted bitter and her heart tugged for him. 'A mistake that forced her to marry my father. A mistake she always made me pay for.'

'But your father loved her, didn't he?' She scanned her

mind for the little snippets of his life he'd told her about, trying to piece things together.

'And that love was rewarded with my being ignored as a young boy.' Pain resounded in his voice and he sighed and turned to look out to sea.

He was turning his back not only on her but on the conversation. It was what he always did, she realised. Right from that first time in his office when he'd looked out over London. It seemed a lifetime ago instead of less than a week.

'But your father moved on and you have a brother now.'

She heard him inhale deeply, saw his shoulders lift and then fall. She'd said the wrong thing again.

'Half-brother.' The words were grated out, and still he kept his back resolutely turned. 'One who has just proved how little he thinks of me. Just as always, he's got what he wants.'

Georgina thought again of all Emma had told her about Carlo. 'I'm sure it's not like that. In fact I'd go as far as to say he doesn't want to inherit the business. He wants to do his own thing, make his own way in life.'

Santos turned round to face her, questions in his dark eyes. 'You're wrong. How could any man not want to inherit his father's business?'

'Not everyone is as motivated by power as you are, Santos. Carlo and Emma just want to make a life together—a normal life.' Without thinking she reached out and touched his arm, her fingers heating as they felt the firmness of his muscles.

'What is that, Georgina?' He sounded drained and tired.

'They want to be together. They're in love, Santos. Is that so hard to accept?' She moved closer to him, trying to quash the surge of love she felt for him as he opened up and let her see his pain.

He looked down into her eyes, his darkening. She thought he might kiss her as he moved closer, with his head dropping lower. But then he stopped, the abruptness of it sending a chill through her.

'No, Georgina, no.' He moved away from her and for the first time ever he looked at a loss for what to say.

This powerful all-controlling man that she'd fallen in love with couldn't and wouldn't accept that love even existed. If that didn't staunch the love that was rapidly growing for him, then nothing would.

'No to what, Santos? Can't you just accept that they love one another and there aren't any ulterior motives at work?'

He changed as he stepped away, as if the distance was enabling him to regain his power, his authority. 'You engineered this whole thing—encouraged them to fly off to Vegas, kept me busy in the way only a woman of your reputation can, and secured a big financial settlement for yourself along the way.'

Hurt raced through her, stinging like a thousand bees. 'You can keep your money, tear up the agreement—anything.' She rounded on him, angry at herself for feeling for him, for wanting to reach out to him, for wanting to love him. 'I don't even know why you haven't just bought Carlo out. It would have been much less complicated than getting married.'

'Don't insult my business management. You know nothing about it—about the way Carlo has refused my generous offer, not once but twice, holding out for the ultimate prize.'

His voice was fierce but she didn't pay any heed to it

at all. Her emotions were running so high she no longer cared what happened.

'No, I *don't* know anything about it. All I know is that I should never have got involved.' She hissed the words at him as his dark eyes accused her. 'I should have just helped them get married.'

'You did.'

'No!' Exasperation made her voice sharp.

He really believed she'd done this for money, for her own gain as well as Emma's. Enraged beyond comprehension, she marched to his study. Her thoughts were beyond rational as she barged into the room, and when she saw the file holding their agreement on his desk she picked it up.

Santos entered the study just as she took hold of the agreement they'd both signed such a short time ago, his face as dark as the thunderclouds had been earlier. She looked at him, smiled sarcastically. Challenging him. Then she tore up the agreement into as many tiny pieces as her shaking hands could manage.

'You can do what you like, *mi esposa*, but you will still be my wife.'

'I'm leaving, Santos, as your wife or not. I don't care, but I'm going back to London.'

She pushed past him and almost ran to her room. Without pausing she grabbed her handbag, checked for her passport and spun on her heel, not wanting anything from him.

She'd get a taxi to the airport and sit there all night if she had to, but one thing was for sure: she'd be on the next flight back to London. With that plan of action in mind she headed for the front door of the villa, glad Santos was nowhere to be seen.

Anger and frustration still raced in her veins as she pulled open the heavy ornate door—but Santos stood there, hands folded across his powerful body.

CHAPTER ELEVEN

'I HAVE TO go, Santos,' she fired at him, her heart thudding so loudly she thought he might hear it. 'We should never have married. I was stupid to think it could work.'

'Stupid to try and deceive me—that's what you mean, is it not, *querida*?' His words were slow and very deliberate.

The setting sun cast an orange glow around him as he stood firm and resolute before her. Despite the pain in her heart, her body responded to the image of him—the man she loved. The man she must never think of again once she'd got back to London. Perhaps she'd move away, get a small place in the country, live simply and quietly. Anything not to have to see him again.

'I'm not even going to deny it.' Her temper flared. 'You're determined to think the worst so you can go ahead and do it, just like you have with your brother and his mother. Even your father.'

He inhaled deeply, his handsome face becoming sharper than she'd ever seen. His eyes hardened until they resembled polished obsidian, with glittering hints of the lava that formed it hidden in their depths.

'Get in the car, Georgina.' His tone brooked no rebuke and she stiffened at the challenge. There was no way she was going to let him stop her. She had to get away—as far away as possible.

'No,' she said vehemently, and tried to move past him, but his reactions were fast and he instantly blocked her, his dominating body filling the doorway.

'I'm going to the airport.'

'Then I shall take you.' His tone was as overpowering as his body.

She looked from his face to the car behind him and noticed for the first time that the passenger door was open and the engine running. Her heart raced at the thought of being with him for just a little while longer, because despite everything that was where she wanted to be. But he would never want her as his wife now—not when he believed her capable of such deception. A deception she was innocent of.

'Why?' She couldn't help herself asking, as if in just a few seconds he would have changed his mind about her.

'You are my wife, and as such I will drive you to the airport.'

He left her in no doubt that there wouldn't be any further discussion on the subject and she dropped down into the low sports car, nerves taking flight in her stomach as he climbed into the driver's seat.

She glanced across at him as the air inside the car filled with his raw masculine scent—one that would haunt her for ever—only to find he was looking at her. Furiously she glared at him, then looked away. She wasn't going to be a victim of his charm this time. The sooner she got to the airport the better.

The drive along the busy roads was fast and painfully silent. Each time she looked at him his stern profile hinted at the anger he held in check. Each passing second became tenser than the last, the air more laden and heavy, and she breathed a sigh of relief as the airport came into view.

He passed the entrance and she panicked. 'Where are we going?'

'My plane is waiting on the Tarmac.'

'You don't need to do that. I'll book on the next flight.' She tried hard to keep her desperation from him, but it wasn't just him she was annoyed with. She'd almost hoped he was coming to London too and that he did want her.

'We shall be in London by midnight.'

'We?' She silently cursed that last thought—that last futile wish.

'Did you really think you could walk out so easily?' He turned to look at her briefly as he manoeuvred the car into the airport and headed for the plane. Within seconds of them stopping he was out of the car and at her door, and once their passports were checked he took her hand and led her up the steps of the plane.

The door closed and a strange stillness settled inside the cabin. Santos sat in one of the white leather chairs, his long legs stretched out before him, looking relaxed, but she knew from the tension in his face he was anything but.

Georgina resigned herself to the situation and sat down, fixing her attention on the darkening skyline rather than look at the man who'd turned everything in her life upside down, including her heart. She consoled herself with the fact that at least she was going back to London. Once there she could so much more easily walk away from Santos. But that thought didn't make her feel as she'd wanted it to. It made her heart ache. Pain lanced through it, shattering it into pieces. But she couldn't let him know.

* * *

If Santos had thought the flight to London was tense, then the drive through London's streets was worse. Georgina sat at his side, irresistibly close, yet undeniably far from him. He knew she was trapped in her deceit. The evidence was stacked against her. She'd deceived him, tricked him into marrying her so her sister and his brother could take all he'd worked so hard for over recent years. This time Georgina's gamble wasn't going to pay off.

'I can't stay here.'

Georgina's words drew him up sharp. She'd realised where they were. The storm, it seemed, raged on.

'Take me back to my own apartment, please.'

He didn't say anything, just shook his head once as she looked across at him, her face partially lit by street lamps.

'Santos, please, don't prolong the agony.'

The anguish in her voice was so acute it was almost physical. But what did she mean, agony? Had their time together been so awful?

'Agony? What agony?' he snapped at her recklessly, instantly furious with himself for allowing her to see even a moment's loss of control.

She looked taken aback, as if she hadn't meant to say those words. 'Just admit it's time we went our separate ways, Santos. Things haven't worked out.' She hesitated for a moment as the car pulled up outside his apartment. 'We've both been deceived—let's leave it at that.' She sounded tired, as if struggling with defeat.

'You are my wife, Georgina, and as such I want you with me when Carlo and Emma return. I want us to present a united front.' He couldn't admit it yet—not even to himself—but he seemed to be clutching at every possible reason for her to stay, as if he didn't want her to go.

The chauffeur opened the car door and he stepped out

into the cold autumn night. Light rain had fallen and the small amount of traffic that passed swished by on the wet road. He walked round to the other side of the car and opened Georgina's door, marvelling at how suddenly she seemed at ease. Was he even now falling into line with one of her devious plans?

She stepped out onto the pavement and looked at him. 'I don't see why we should keep up the pretence any longer.'

'No?' He walked towards the entrance doors, glancing back and hoping she would follow. He wasn't in the mood for any more in-depth discussions. 'Do you not want to continue until Emma comes back? It would be better if she thought you were happy, would it not?'

He watched as her expression changed from defiance to realisation that he spoke the truth. He certainly didn't want Carlo to think he'd married Georgina in a bid to secure the business; it was an ongoing issue between them. One that now threatened everything he'd ever cared about.

'You're right.' She sighed and smiled sweetly at him—a little too sweetly, convincing him that even now she played the game, using him as she had from the very beginning. 'It wouldn't do if they found out what we'd done—for reasons other than love, of course.'

Opening the door, he walked towards the lift, pressed the button and turned to her. Did she *have* to keep brandishing that word about? As if it was the very centre of everything that had happened?

Irritated, he looked above the lift doors, anxious to see if it was coming. 'It will be for the best,' he said tersely.

'That's debatable,' she tossed at him as the lift doors opened and she walked in. 'I've yet to decide just who it will be best for, but tonight, at least, I'm prepared to stay here.'

He didn't know what to say to that—his usual quick thinking had totally deserted him—so he remained silent as the lift took them up to his apartment, acutely aware of her so very close to him. He could smell her sweet floral scent and clenched his hands into fists in a bid to stamp out the threatening fire.

Santos unlocked the door and Georgina couldn't believe she was back at his apartment. Everything she'd planned had gone wrong and, worse, had been for nothing. She'd told Santos she could have just encouraged Emma and Carlo to run off and get married and now she wished she had. At least then she wouldn't have tasted something she could never have. She wouldn't have fallen in love with a man who openly admitted he wasn't capable of love in any form.

She sighed wearily. The last few days had been emotionally challenging for all the wrong reasons and she just wanted to be on her own.

'It's late,' she said softly as he flicked on the lights in the kitchen. 'I'm going straight to bed.'

She looked across at him, wanting to add that she was going alone, that she would spend the night in the same room she'd occupied before, but something in his expression held her back. Her heart began to race as the intensity of his gaze rested on her, as if he too couldn't bring himself to suggest she sleep alone.

He walked towards her, his footsteps echoing on the wooden floor, and like an animal caught in car headlights she just stood there and watched, mesmerised by him. Nerves made her bite gently on her bottom lip as he stopped in front of her, so close and yet so far.

'Where are you going to sleep, *mi esposa*? With your husband or alone?'

His accent had become more defined, sending shivers of awareness all over her. When his gaze rested on her lips she stopped biting them and smiled, almost tasting the saccharine of it.

'Alone.'

With you, her mind screamed as that one word left her lips. She wanted to sleep beside the man she loved, feel the warmth of his body next to her. But she reminded herself the man she loved didn't really exist. That man had been pretence and nothing more. This was the real Santos.

'Then I shall say *buenas noches, mi esposa.*'

He moved closer. Instinct told her he was going to kiss her, and heaven help her she wanted him to, but if he did…

She stepped back. 'Goodnight, Santos,' she said as firmly as possible, before retreating to the safety of the room she'd previously occupied.

Santos watched her go, confusion racing through him. Why was he trying to prevent her from leaving? Just what kind of power did she have over him? Perhaps it was better if they slept alone—although his body protested at the idea. He knew he needed time to think. He had to be sure of what to do next and at the moment he hadn't a clue.

With an exasperated sigh he tousled his hair and turned on his heel. Strong coffee was what he needed. And work. Going to an empty bed when Georgina slept in the next room was not going to be an option. Neither was going to her and trying to explain—to himself as well as her—why he didn't want her to go.

The aroma of fresh coffee lingered in the air, and

the taste of it invigorated his senses as he headed for his study. He had reports to catch up on and an aching need to deny.

A neatly stacked pile of post almost made him groan aloud. He wasn't in the mood. But as he sat at his desk the postmark on one letter caught his attention. A solicitor's name glared out at him from the large white envelope. Anxiously he tore it open, but was totally unprepared for what he saw.

So unprepared he had to read it again.

Carlo had renounced all claims to his father's estate in deference to him. Santos closed his eyes in relief, but that was short-lived as the implications of the letter hit home. What would this mean for him and Georgina?

He tried to get Carlo on his mobile, but it went straight to voicemail. Annoyed, he hung up. He wasn't about to leave a message. Instead he tried to focus on his work, but all sorts of jumbled thoughts raced through his mind. He'd never felt this disorientated or distracted before.

After several hours he gave up on trying to work or contacting Carlo. He picked up the letter again and headed for the kitchen, unable even to consider trying to sleep. More coffee was required. As it brewed he read the letter again, trying to understand why his brother had felt the need to do this when he'd offered to buy him out several times. What point was he making?

Exasperated, he tossed it on the kitchen table and walked over to the windows. The faint light of dawn crept across the sky, and with it he hoped would come answers and solutions.

It was still very early, but Georgina knew that Santos was likely to be up and about, so she quickly scanned the living room, relieved to see it empty, and headed for the kitchen. She flicked on the kettle and searched for a mug, needing as much caffeine as she could get after her sleepless night. She noticed the partly drunk cups of cold coffee—evidence that either Santos had been entertaining or he too had had a bad night.

The coffee's aroma revived her and she leant back against one of the kitchen units to sip her drink, wrapping her hands comfortingly around her mug. It was then that she noticed the letter. It looked official, and at first she turned the other way, but as she did so a name caught her attention.

She looked more closely and nearly gasped at what she saw. The letter very clearly stated that Carlo had renounced his claim on his father's estate.

Guilt rushed through her for even thinking of looking at Santos's mail, but that was hotly followed by anger and disappointment. This letter changed everything. Santos would inherit his father's business without the need for a wife—or an heir. He didn't need her any more. So why was he tormenting her like this? Insisting she stay with him? To punish her?

She should feel relieved. At least she could walk away from him and try and piece together her life. Emma had Carlo and didn't need her any more, so she could get that longed-for peaceful cottage in the country.

The coffee turned bitter in her mouth and she put the nearly full mug down on the side, turning her back on the letter and all it meant. She felt sick when she should be relieved that she could at last walk away from this sham of a marriage. She should be heading out of the door right now and not giving the man she'd married a second thought. But she couldn't.

She couldn't just walk away.

She loved him.

'They're back.'

Santos's voice broke through her rambling thoughts. His hair was still damp from the shower. The last time she'd seen his hair wet they had just shared the most amazing moment in the shower. Did he remember that? She looked at him, as immaculate as ever in his designer suit, and found it hard to believe he would.

'Are they all right?' She pushed aside her memories and worries as she watched him walk past her into the kitchen. She was mesmerised by him, by the powerful aura he exuded, and found all she could do was watch as he organised fresh coffee.

'Of course they are. We'll have dinner with them tonight. Sort everything out.'

He sounded cheerful, not at all weighed down by the problems of the last few days. That letter had obviously made everything right for *him*, but when was he going to tell *her*? Then it hit her. How long had he known?

'No.'

The word rang out in the kitchen and he stopped and looked at her, a frown creasing his brow.

'I can't.'

'Don't you want to see Emma? I thought it would be what you wanted?' He looked puzzled. He flicked the switch on the coffee machine and walked over to her. 'What's the matter, Georgina?'

The concern that should have been in such words was missing, replaced by suspicion.

She bit down hard on her tongue. She wanted to tell him she knew about the letter, wanted to demand to know when he'd known about it. But as she looked up into his face, searched his eyes, all she could do was shake her head.

He reached out to her, holding her arms loosely, and

looked at her. 'What's wrong?' And this time he did sound concerned—but not for her, surely?

Wrong? *Everything* was wrong. And suddenly she knew she couldn't walk away from him without telling him why.

'You wouldn't understand.' She dropped her gaze, not able to bear his scrutiny any longer. And if he turned on the charm she'd never resist, never be able to explain anything.

'I could try.' His voice wasn't as firm as usual, and a waver of doubt lingered in it.

'No, Santos, you couldn't. You don't do love. You don't know how it feels to love someone so much you'd do anything for them, only to find they've deceived you.' The floodgates had opened and the words tumbled out as she looked up at him again, her eyes begging him to understand.

He let go of her arms and stepped back a pace, his tall, athletic body dominating her, as big a hurdle for her to overcome as the shock of seeing the letter.

'Don't do this to yourself, Georgina.'

'What do you want me to do? Shut myself away from love just like you have?'

He stood, immovable and silent as she waited for him to say something. Finally he spoke. 'You're right. I don't understand.'

She closed her eyes for a second against the pain of his admission, then opened them and looked at him, injecting as much firmness into her voice as possible. 'There's no reason for us to be together any more, Santos.' She hesitated as she saw the firm set of his shoulders. 'I'm going home.'

'Leaving, you mean?'

She watched his jaw clench as he stood, all but blocking her way out of the room.

'Yes, leaving.' She walked past him into the living area, her arm brushing his as she did so. The shock of that contact made her take in a sharp breath.

Santos clenched his hands into tight fists and bit down hard. He wanted to tell her to stay, but he didn't know how to—let alone why. Was it because not only was she the first woman who hadn't succumbed to his charm immediately, but the first woman to walk out on him?

But she *wasn't* the first woman to walk out on him. His mother had done the same. He'd stood and watched her leave, not understanding why. He'd felt helpless then too.

'Georgina.'

Her name snapped from his lips and for a moment he wondered if he'd actually spoken, then he heard her footsteps stop. Ominous silence filled the apartment.

He took in a deep breath and left the kitchen. She stood by the front door. Last time she'd tried to walk out on him he'd gone with her, but this time he couldn't. This time all he could do was watch her go. He couldn't risk opening his heart to her.

She raised her brows at him in question. She wouldn't even speak to him. Should he ask her to stay? Tell her he wanted to understand? That somewhere deep inside he was beginning to understand that elusive emotion love?

But still he couldn't.

'My solicitor will contact you with regard to the divorce.'

CHAPTER TWELVE

GEORGINA HELD THE letter in shaking hands. Santos hadn't wasted any time. He must have instructed his solicitor to file for divorce the moment she'd left his apartment. But what had she expected? That he would miss her? Come after her and declare his undying love?

He'd admitted that he didn't understand. They'd been almost his last words to her that morning.

Well, if he thought she'd hide away and meekly sign the papers then he had another thought coming. She would show him she could be as strong as he was. She would go down fighting. Fighting for the love she couldn't deny herself but had to.

With that in mind she tapped in to the same fiery determination that had given her the courage to march into his office and suggest they marry in the first place.

She put on her charcoal suit, her high heels and applied make-up. Then she pulled out her rarely used briefcase, put the letter inside and left, slamming the front door behind her. The few persistent photographers waiting intently outside her flat almost fazed her—they'd been camping out since the details of their marriage had hit the headlines, desperate for a story—but she passed through them, refusing to answer their questions or make a comment, quickly hailing a taxi.

By the time the taxi pulled up outside the Ramirez International offices it had started to rain, but she refused to rush in, head down against the rain. With her head held high she walked determinedly in, hardly giving the rain a second thought. Alone inside the lift she had time to check her appearance. It was vital she looked as sleek and sophisticated as possible. He must never know how devastated she was by the last two weeks, how little sleep she'd had recently.

She smoothed her hands down her skirt, took a deep breath and walked proudly out of the lift as soon as the doors opened. His secretary looked up as she pushed open the heavy glass door, but Georgina wasn't about to stop and ask permission to see her husband. He was going to listen to what she had say whether he liked it or not.

'Excuse me, Miss…' the shocked woman said as she made her way straight towards Santos's office.

Georgina stopped and turned to face her. 'It's Mrs,' she said firmly. 'Mrs Ramirez. And I'm here to see my husband.'

With that she turned and walked down the wide corridor that led to his office. Nothing was going to stop her now.

She paused briefly outside the door, her hand poised above the handle. Last time she'd stood there full of nerves, hardly able to believe she was about to propose to a man she'd never met.

Not for one minute had she thought she would find him so devastatingly attractive. And if she'd known that from the very first moment their eyes met a sizzle of desire would weave a spell so strong about them she would have turned and run, regardless of her motives.

She'd never expected to fall in love with him so quickly and so completely.

It had taken the letter instigating their divorce this morning for her to realise what she had to do—that she couldn't run any more. She'd stood by and watched two men she'd loved in very different ways from the way she loved Santos leave her. This time she was determined it would be different. This time she wouldn't shrink from the pain. This time she'd face it head-on.

She took a deep breath, gathered all her nerve and opened the door.

He was sitting at his desk, looking cool and composed. Her heart lurched just at seeing him, but she couldn't let that get the better of her now.

'To what do I owe this pleasure?'

His words were as cool and clear as a mountain stream but she couldn't falter now.

She put her briefcase on his desk, looked him in the eye and flicked it open. The dark depths of his eyes glittered as he watched every slow, purposeful movement. Taking out the letter, she placed it on the desk and then closed her briefcase.

'Don't play games, Santos. You know why I'm here. To put an end to our marriage.'

But not until he knew how she felt—knew she loved him. But telling someone who hated even to hear the word, let alone acknowledge the emotion, wasn't going to be easy.

He stood up, his height as intimidating as the breadth of his shoulders, but she held his gaze, trying hard to ignore the lurching of her heart.

'A marriage *you* instigated, Georgina. Here, in this very room.'

Santos moved from behind his desk and came closer to her, even now unable to resist the challenge her eyes fired at him. The first time she'd stood in his office, with fire and determination burning in her eyes, he'd wanted her.

He still wanted her. The force of the attraction hadn't lessened after spending the night with her. It had increased.

'One you willingly went along with. You changed it to suit your needs simply to get a business. You didn't think I was worthy of an explanation about the heir you needed to inherit everything.'

Her angry accusation had found its mark but he wouldn't let her see that.

'You make it sound calculated when it wasn't.'

He leant against the edge of his desk, folded his arms across his chest, fighting the urge to tell her everything. Then he remembered the pain in her voice when she'd told him she couldn't have children.

'I had no idea then that you couldn't have children.' His voice sounded unsteady even to him, and she closed her eyes, her long lashes shutting him out. He reached out to her, his hand touching her arm in a gesture of concern. She jumped back from him, her eyes now blazing. 'I'm sorry.'

She remained silent, her steady gaze holding his, and he wished she'd let him close. He'd never meant to hurt her. She had made him feel things he'd never thought he would. He still found it hard to comprehend the aching void in his life, an ache born out of love. But now she hated him.

'It's not that I *can't* have children, Santos.'

She spoke in a harsh, raw tone, her words snagging his conscience.

'I just couldn't bring a child into the world for that reason. I would have thought you of all people would understand that.'

His mind roared as the pain of his childhood rushed back at him. He'd been a mistake. One that had forced his mother into marriage with a man she couldn't love. With dreadful clarity he realised Georgina was right. If he'd had to he would have resorted to fathering a child just to get the business—a child that he didn't want. But wasn't that why he'd never married? To avoid such a decision?

Guilt slashed at him, making his next words harsh and serrated.

'If I could have avoided that I would have done.'

'The same as you could have avoided all this.' She pointed fiercely at the letter which lay on her briefcase. 'If you'd just talked to Carlo he wouldn't have had to go to the extremes he did. You denied Emma her big day.' She paused for a moment, her dark eyes flecked with gold sparks of determination. 'You should still talk to Carlo.'

Again she was right, and he gritted his teeth angrily. Talking to Carlo hadn't been an option before, but he could put that right. With an exasperated sigh he thrust himself away from the desk and strode towards the windows. Raindrops ran down them, diluting the view of London.

'Don't hide from it, Santos. You used me to score points on your own brother.'

The accusation flew at him but he kept his back resolutely to her. She made him feel exposed, vulnerable. Damn it, she made him feel emotions he didn't want— emotions he didn't need.

He turned to face her, and despite the hardness of her expression he saw the pain on her face, felt it radiating out.

'I was caught up in battle started by my mother. On her deathbed she made me promise never to let go of what was rightfully mine. When you so calmly offered marriage I never meant it to go any further.'

She made a sound that was a mixture of a gasp and a whimper—a sound full of pain. 'So seducing me, getting me into your bed, was a mistake too?'

He watched the rapid rise and fall of her chest and realised she wasn't nearly as rational as she wanted him to believe. 'No, Georgina,' he said as he moved towards her, his tone lower and huskier just from his memories of that night. 'I wanted you then as much as you wanted me.'

She blushed, and it shocked him to realise how he'd missed that innocent blush.

'I hate you for that.'

She hated him.

The venom in her voice left him in no doubt that she meant it and something changed inside him—as if somewhere a key had turned, unlocking something, some sort of emotion he wasn't yet ready for.

'Don't play the wounded party with me when you already have one very convenient marriage behind you.' Anger was the best line of defence. It would supress whatever it was she'd unlocked, because right now was not the time to analyse it.

'Richard never forced me into his bed. He didn't seduce me and I love him for that.'

Her words rang loud and clear in his head, as if she were at the top of a bell tower.

Santos gritted his teeth against those words. She'd loved Richard. It was as if he'd stepped back a few decades—as if he was witnessing the love his father and stepmother had shared, a love that had excluded him. But that exclusion hadn't made him feel raw with the pain he now felt.

'So you openly admit you married him for money?' He maintained his angry defence—anything other than accept what the raging pain inside him might mean.

'Yes, I did!' She flung the words at him. 'He asked

me, he saw I needed help and offered it, but I had no idea then just how ill he was. That's why he insisted I marry him—because he knew it was the only way to be sure he could provide for me into the future.'

He didn't want to hear it, yet at the same time he did.

Her face softened. 'He loved me, and for the chance he gave me I loved him.'

Santos was consumed with jealousy. He couldn't hear anything else other than that she'd loved Richard.

Georgina watched as Santos's face hardened. He couldn't even stand to hear the word *love*—couldn't contemplate such an emotion existed. He'd been denied it as a child and now, as an adult, he was determined to continue to deny himself.

She knew she was taunting him, using that word again, but she pressed on, hoping he'd see how she felt. 'I loved him in a compassionate way. There wasn't even a flicker of a spark of passion. It was a comfortable love. A safe love. Not the way I love you.'

Silence stretched between them. She remained tall and straight, even though she wanted to crumple on the floor right in front of him. The silence lengthened.

She shouldn't have said anything—shouldn't have opened her heart to his ridicule. Not when she knew how he scorned love. A lump gathered in her throat, almost choking her. This was no different from watching her father walk away. No different from having to say goodbye to Richard. As if her love had made them leave. She knew it wasn't true, but the pain of it had made it feel that way.

Fear of going through that again was what drove her now. It was why she'd come here—why she was exposing herself so utterly to Santos's contempt. If she was yet again to lose a man she loved, she was going to make her feelings clear.

'Do you really expect me to believe that when these last weeks have been nothing but a big lie, an act for you?' His words were sharp, heightening the tension between them.

'It wasn't a lie. There were times…' She paused, feeling heat spread across her cheeks as she remembered their wedding night, the passion they'd shared. That night there hadn't been any pretence, any acting on her part. She swallowed hard and continued. 'There were times when it was real.'

'Would that be the moment you kissed me at the party, or the morning you all but seduced me into staying on the yacht? Or the times when all your acting skills were called upon so that you could cover for Emma and Carlo running off to get married?'

The cynicism in his voice lashed at her like hail, each word stinging. How could he still believe she had had any part in it?

'I had no part whatsoever in their marriage,' she fumed at him, frustration rising like a spring tide. 'They deceived me too, Santos.' She stood facing him across the office, the expanse of soft cream carpet seeming to grow bigger between them with every passing second. 'They were desperate.'

'Back to that again, are we?'

Each word was like a bullet in her heart, each one wounding her further.

'I can see that whatever I say won't make any difference to you, Santos. You're incapable of love.'

'I made that perfectly clear from our very first meeting.'

In exasperation she covered her face with her hands

briefly, dropped her head and took in a long, shuddering breath. She couldn't take it any more, and gave vent to her frustration. 'You're so cold, so proud, and so damned stubborn. It was a mistake coming here.'

She pulled her jacket tighter about her body, as if it would deflect the hurt. For a moment his gaze lowered, caught by the movement. He took a step closer to her, his eyes meeting hers once more. She stepped back instinctively, needing space to be able to think.

'So why *did* you come, *mi esposa*? Tell me. Why?'

His accent became heavy and to her dismay he moved closer still, rendering thought almost impossible.

She whirled round and grabbed the papers from his desk, knocking her briefcase to the floor in the process. 'To sign these.' She waved the papers at him furiously. 'To put an end to something that should never have been started.'

'You could have sent them via your solicitor.' His calm voice irritated her further.

'And I wish I had. But I was taking a chance—a gamble.' She watched as he frowned, his dark eyes narrowing. 'I had to know.'

He said nothing, as if he was trying to take in what she said, so she dropped the papers on the desk purposefully, picked up a pen and signed, tossing the pen back onto the polished surface next to the papers.

'And now I do.'

Santos watched her sign the papers, listened as the pen crashed to the table. Each breath was hard to take, as if he was being suffocated. He hurt. Pain raced through him.

Even as she walked across the office he couldn't say a word, couldn't move, as if he'd been frozen in time. What the hell was the matter with him?

Something snapped, as if chains had broken. He inhaled deeply. The noise caught her attention and she turned to look at him. Her face was pale.

'I know I was a fool.' She threw the words at him as if he was nothing more than dirt at the edge of the road. 'I gambled and I lost.'

He tried to make sense of her words. What was she trying to tell him?

Not the way I love you.

His mind replayed what she'd said moments before. Purposefully he moved towards her, and when she turned again panic tore through him. If she left now he'd never see her again. He couldn't let her go. Not yet. He loved her; he'd just refused to admit it.

'I gambled too.'

The words hurried out and he clenched his hands, trying to keep himself from reaching for her, from preventing her from leaving.

She spun round and faced him again, her eyes sparkling with molten gold. 'Not with emotions, you didn't.'

She moved towards the door so suddenly he was taken off guard.

'You gambled with your brother's happiness, your greed. You won, Santos, and I hope you're happy.'

Happy? He was the furthest thing from happy. He hadn't felt like this since the day his mother had calmly left, saying goodbye as if she was just going shopping.

'Georgina.'

He tried to form the words, tried to tell her he hadn't gambled with Carlo's happiness—at least not intentionally. He wanted to tell her he'd gambled his own—and hers. Something he hadn't even realised until just a few seconds ago.

'Don't, Santos. I don't want to hear how you're driven by power and the need to control everything.'

'That may have been true once.' The words rushed out and for the first time in his adult life he knew he was losing.

'And it still is.' Her words were softer now, as if she'd given up fighting.

Mutely he watched as she opened the office door and paused in the doorway.

'Goodbye, Santos.'

His reaction was so swift he didn't have time to think. All he wanted to do was stop her from leaving, from walking out of his life for good. A life that wouldn't be the same once she'd gone.

He reached out and took hold of her arm, propelling her back into the room, and kicked the door shut on the enquiring glances of passing staff. She looked up at him, her brown eyes wide, darkening rapidly, her breathing hard and fast. But it was the current of pure electricity between them that told him he was doing the right thing.

He didn't want her to go. It wasn't possession. It wasn't power. It was more than that.

It was love.

He loved her.

This passionate woman had unlocked his heart, healed his wounds and shown him how love could be. He'd just been too stubborn to realise.

Georgina stepped back as he let her go, watching the show of emotions cross his handsome face. His pain and confusion were palpable, and she wanted to reach out to him—but to do so would be her undoing. Again she stepped back, but he moved closer until she had nowhere to go, the wall against her back.

'This is what you do to me.' His voice was hoarse with emotion. 'I can't think around you. I can't sleep without you by my side. I can't let you go.'

Her heart fluttered wildly and she dragged in a ragged breath. 'Santos…?' His name was barely a whisper from her lips.

He placed his palm on the wall above her shoulder, his face coming closer to hers, bringing him irresistibly close. Too close.

'I want you, Georgina,' he said huskily as he lowered his head to kiss her.

She moved sideways, away from temptation, but instantly he placed his other hand above her shoulder. Trapping her.

'I want you with a passion so raw it almost hurts. In fact it does.'

She looked up into his dark eyes, so close now she could see how enlarged his pupils were, see the desire swirling there.

Say it, her mind urged him, but she refused to utter the words aloud. The blood rushed in her ears as her heart thumped and she bit her bottom lip hard. She would never beg anyone to say it. If he loved her he had to tell her.

'I've never known this before, Georgina.'

'What?' she asked in a timid whisper, hardly daring to hear the answer.

'Love.'

Her heart sang as he rubbed the pad of his thumb over her lips, easing the pain where she'd bitten into them hard.

'I've never met a woman like you. From the moment you walked in here my fate was sealed. I just didn't know it then. I couldn't admit it—not even to myself.'

'Can you now?' she said in a cracked whisper.

He took her in his arms, pulled her close against him. 'I love you, Georgina. My heart belongs to you and I never want it back.'

Her knees weakened and his arms tightened around her as he brushed his lips over hers. She pushed against his chest so she could look into his eyes. 'I love you, Santos.'

With that he claimed her lips in a kiss so passionate it took all her breath away, leaving her light-headed.

'Can we start again? Begin our marriage now, with honesty and love?'

As she looked up into the handsome face of the man she loved sunbeams lit up the office, casting a glow all around them. Once again the storm was over—and this time it was for good.

'Only if it means we get another wedding night,' she teased.

He laughed gently. 'Now, *that* I can promise you, *mi esposa.*'

EPILOGUE

THE LEAVES WERE turning all shades of gold and brown as Georgina looked around the country cottage garden. Autumn sun cast its last lazy glow as it slid slowly behind the hill.

'Happy anniversary,' Santos said softly as he came to stand behind her.

He wrapped his arms around her. She leant back against him, happier than she'd ever been.

'You've brought me to the country for our anniversary weekend?' She hadn't doubted he'd remember their first anniversary—she just hadn't expected him to help her realise one of her dreams, even if it was only for a weekend. It would be a wonderful place to give him her gift.

'I've done more than that, Georgie.' He nuzzled her hair and then kissed her head. 'I've bought you this piece of the English countryside. This place is yours.'

Georgina swivelled round in his arms and looked up at him, excitement almost exploding inside her. 'This place? You've bought it?'

'I most certainly have, and now is your chance to show me just what is so wonderful about living in the countryside.'

'Oh, Santos, it's perfect.'

She couldn't believe that this cottage, with roses ram-

bling around the front door, was all hers. He opened the
door and led her inside. It had been furnished and deco-
rated to the highest standard, just as she would have expected from Santos, but it still maintained that country
charm she'd always longed for.

'In fact it's more than perfect.'

'There's more, *mi esposa*.'

'What more could there be than this?'

'Emma and Carlo will be joining us.'

'They will?'

'It's their anniversary too, and I thought it would be
nice to be together, but we still have a few hours before they arrive. Carlo has become a workaholic since he
opened his own hotel, and he wouldn't leave until he'd
sorted everything out for the weekend.'

Georgina laughed at the image of her brother-in-law
putting the business before a weekend with Emma. 'Perhaps there is more of you in him than you realise?' she
teased, and reached up to brush a kiss on his lips.

'Well, you should know what we Ramirez men are
like by now.'

He kissed her and passion sparked to life, zipping between them.

She pulled back from him and looked into his eyes,
which were darkening by the second. 'I have a gift for
you too.'

He put her at arm's length and smiled. 'Can you beat
this?' he asked as he took her into the living room, which
looked cosy and inviting.

'You're going to be a father.'

'Are you serious?' He looked deep into her eyes,
studying her reaction.

She nodded, unable say anything. After years of telling herself she'd be the worst mother a child could have, she was still apprehensive.

'When?' His words seemed choked and hard to come by.

'You're impatient, aren't you?' she teased gently.

'Not impatient. Overjoyed. And very much in love with you.' He kissed her softly and with so much love she fought back the tears of happiness that threatened.

'April,' she said as his lips left hers. 'Our baby will be born in April.'

'That,' he said huskily as he smiled down at her, 'is a cause for celebration.'

She laughed and snuggled against him, relishing the strength of his arms around her. 'I love you so much, Santos,' she said as she heard his heartbeat.

He swept her off her feet and, looking down at her, smiled. 'I'm the happiest man alive and it's all thanks to you. How did I ever manage to exist before you arrived in my life?'

He edged his way out of the living room towards the stairs, a stream of Spanish rushing from his lips as he looked at the narrow staircase.

Georgina laughed.

'Put me down.' She placed her hand on his cheek and kissed him briefly. 'This is one flight of stairs you *won't* be able to carry me up.'

* * * * *

MILLS & BOON®

Why not subscribe?

Never miss a title and save money too!

Here's what's available to you if you join the exclusive **Mills & Boon Book Club** today:

◆ *Titles up to a month ahead of the shops*
◆ *Amazing discounts*
◆ *Free P&P*
◆ *Earn Bonus Book points that can be redeemed against other titles and gifts*
◆ *Choose from monthly or pre-paid plans*

Still want more?

Well, if you join today we'll even give you
50% OFF your first parcel!

So visit **www.millsandboon.co.uk/subs**
or call **Customer Relations** on **020 8288 2888**
to be a part of this exclusive Book Club!

Snow, sleigh bells and a hint of seduction

Find your perfect Christmas reads at
millsandboon.co.uk/Christmas

MILLS & BOON®

Why shop at millsandboon.co.uk?

Each year, thousands of romance readers find their perfect read at millsandboon.co.uk. That's because we're passionate about bringing you the very best romantic fiction. Here are some of the advantages of shopping at www.millsandboon.co.uk:

* **Get new books first**—you'll be able to buy your favourite books one month before they hit the shops

* **Get exclusive discounts**—you'll also be able to buy our specially created monthly collections, with up to 50% off the RRP

* **Find your favourite authors**—latest news, interviews and new releases for all your favourite authors and series on our website, plus ideas for what to try next

* **Join in**—once you've bought your favourite books, don't forget to register with us to rate, review and join in the discussions

Visit **www.millsandboon.co.uk**
for all this and more today!